GOOSEBUMPS HorrorLand™
ALL-NEW, ALL-TERRIFYING

#1 REVENGE OF THE LIVING DUMMY
Also Available on Audiobook from Scholastic Audiobooks

#2 CREEP FROM THE DEEP
Also Available on Audiobook from Scholastic Audiobooks

#3 MONSTER BLOOD FOR BREAKFAST!

#4 THE SCREAM OF THE HAUNTED MASK

#5 DR. MANIAC VS. ROBBY SCHWARTZ

#6 WHO'S YOUR MUMMY?

#7 MY FRIENDS CALL ME MONSTER

#8 SAY CHEESE — AND DIE SCREAMING!

GOOSEBUMPS®
NOW WITH BONUS FEATURES!
LOOK IN THE BACK OF THE **BOOK**
FOR EXCLUSIVE AUTHOR INTERVIEWS AND MORE.

NIGHT OF THE LIVING DUMMY

DEEP TROUBLE

MONSTER BLOOD

THE HAUNTED MASK

ONE DAY AT HORRORLAND

THE CURSE OF THE MUMMY'S TOMB

BE CAREFUL WHAT YOU WISH FOR

SAY CHEESE AND DIE!

WHO'S YOUR MUMMY?

R.L. STINE

SCHOLASTIC INC.
New York Toronto London Auckland Sydney
Mexico City New Delhi Hong Kong Buenos Aires

No part of this publication may be reproduced, stored in a retrieval system, or transmitted in any form or by any means, electronic, mechanical, photocopying, recording, or otherwise, without written permission of the publisher. For information regarding permission, write to Scholastic Inc., Attention: Permissions Department, 557 Broadway, New York, NY 10012.

ISBN-13: 978-0-439-91874-9
ISBN-10: 0-439-91874-X
Goosebumps book series created by Parachute Press, Inc.

Goosebumps HorrorLand #6: *Who's Your Mummy?*
copyright © 2009 by Scholastic Inc.

12 11 10 9 8 7 6 5 4 3 2 1   9 10 11 12 13 14/0

Printed in the U.S.A.
First printing, January 2009

3 RIDES IN 1!

WHO'S YOUR MUMMY?

1

I knew Granny Vee wasn't feeling well. But I didn't know how sick she was. And of course I didn't know that she was about to send my brother, Peter, and me on the most terrifying trip of our lives.

In one week, Peter and I would be listening to the frightening moans of ancient mummies. And covering our ears against their ugly chants.

But today, we were in Granny Vee's living room, running and ducking behind the furniture, laughing and shouting. "HEYYYYY!" I let out a scream as a cold blast of water hit my forehead.

Peter laughed. "Nice move, Abby. You walked right into it!"

I growled and dropped to my knees behind the green corduroy couch. I wiped the water off my face. Then I checked out the tank on my water blaster. Still half full.

I leaned forward. Tensed and waited with my finger on the plastic trigger.

3

Peter was hiding behind the flowery orange-and-yellow curtains. I could see his white sneakers poking out from the bottom.

I waited . . . waited . . . and let go a long, full blast the second he stepped out. It smacked him in the chest and soaked the front of his T-shirt. He stumbled back to the window. His blaster sent a wild spray up toward the ceiling.

"Are you two having fun?"

We both turned to see Granny Vee step into the room. She waved her black cane in the air. "Is it my mistake?" she asked. "I thought I was in my living room. But I seem to have wandered into a water park."

Peter stepped away from the window and lowered his head. "Sorry," he muttered.

I brushed my wet hair out of my eyes. My hair is long and black and very straight. My best feature. And I don't like having it soaked.

I picked up my water bottle from the coffee table and took a long drink.

"I begged you not to use those water guns in the house," Granny Vee said, peering at us through her thick, square-framed glasses.

"Sorry," Peter repeated.

I did one of my famous long-distance water spits and showered the back of his neck.

He let out a squeal and jumped a mile.

"I win!" I said, pumping my fists high above my head.

"Abby, you're a cheater," Granny Vee said, unable to keep a straight face.

She thinks I'm a riot.

"Cheaters never quit, and a quitter never cheats," Granny Vee said. It was one of her favorite sayings.

"It isn't funny!" Peter grumbled. He pulled the soaked T-shirt off, balled it up angrily, and tossed it at me.

Peter has long, straight black hair, too. He's as skinny as a broom handle and short. He's ten — two years younger than me — but he looks like he's seven or eight. Granny Vee says she can't understand why he doesn't grow more — since he eats enough for ten kids!

I'm nearly a foot taller than he is. Which gives me a real advantage in our water-blaster battles. I don't think he's ever won one. Especially when I use my spectacular water-spitting skills against him.

Peter stuck his tongue out at me. Then he stormed out of the room. He's a sore loser.

"Come sit down, Abby." Granny Vee waved me to the couch. I noticed that she was leaning more heavily on her cane than usual.

Her hair has stayed shiny and black. But that day, I saw long gray streaks poking through. And her skin was very pale, so tight I could see her cheekbones underneath.

She lowered herself beside me and squeezed my hand. Her hand was ice-cold!

"I need to talk to you," she said. She looked down at the floor. "I haven't been feeling well."

Those words sent a shock down the back of my neck. I gasped. Granny Vee is the only family Peter and I have. We've been living with Granny Vee since we were little.

If anything happened to her . . .

She kept her gaze on the floor. I saw her shoulders tremble. She was always the powerhouse in the family. Suddenly, she looked so frail.

"I'm going to check into the hospital for some tests," she said softly.

"Tests?" I cried. "What kind of tests?"

She squeezed my hand again. "It'll be okay." Her voice was a whisper.

"But . . . what about Peter and me?" I asked.

She finally turned to look at me. "I have a nice plan for you," she said. "The two of you are going to stay with your Uncle Jonathan."

I blinked. "Who?"

"Your Uncle Jonathan. He hasn't seen you since you were a baby." She smiled. "He's fun. You'll see."

"Where . . . where does he live?" I asked.

"He lives in an old house in a tiny village in Vermont, called Cranford," Granny Vee said. "It'll be a big change from Boston for you. I think you'll both find it very interesting."

My heart was pounding. There were a million questions I wanted to ask. But I couldn't get them out.

"Jonathan can't wait to see you," Granny Vee said. "I sent him pictures of you and Peter. He was thrilled."

She saw the look on my face.

"You'll like him, Abby. He's a very interesting man. And besides, it's only for two weeks."

"But I'm worried about you, Granny Vee," I said. "Why are you sending us to a faraway village? Shouldn't Peter and I stay close?"

She squeezed the handle of her cane. Her hand was so small and white. "Your cell phone will work in Jonathan's village," she said. "We'll talk all the time. I'm sure it'll be fine."

But it wasn't fine. It wasn't fine at all.

"Hey!" Peter stumbled over his suitcase and nearly knocked me over.

"Watch where you're going," I said.

"*You* watch!" he replied. Very mature. He was grumpy the whole train ride. I guess he was just nervous.

I was, too.

I shielded my eyes against the bright sunlight and gazed around the tiny Cranford train station. We were the only ones on the platform. The ticket booth — a tiny brown-shingled hut — was dark and empty. I heard a cat meowing inside it.

No cars in the tiny dirt parking lot. No cars moving on the narrow street.

"Where is Uncle Jonathan?" Peter asked. "Wasn't he supposed to meet us?"

I shrugged. "Beats me." I left my suitcase and stepped to the end of the wooden platform. I peered up and down the street. "Peter, check this place out. It's unbelievable!"

I suddenly felt as if I'd gone back in time. The tiny village looked like something from hundreds of years ago.

The street was made of worn gray cobblestones. On one side stood a row of tiny houses behind picket fences. The houses were so small and low, they looked like dollhouses.

They were white and had slanting red roofs and dark shutters beside the windows. I tried to see inside the windows, but the curtains were all drawn.

The shops on the other side of the street all had old-fashioned signs above the display windows. I squinted into the sunlight to read them.

One read: FOODE SHOPPE. Another, SMITHY AND SON. A shop with a bunch of colored jars in the window was called APOTHECARY. I think that's another word for drugstore.

"Weird," Peter muttered. "Think there's an electronics store? I need a new iPod."

I snickered. "I don't think so," I said.

In the other direction, I saw a tall green hill. The hill cast a shadow over half the village. A huge house rose up near the top of the hill. It looked like an evil castle from a horror movie, with dark towers on both sides.

I squinted into the sunlight. "Peter — look!" I cried. "What are those creatures flying over that big house up there?" I pointed at the fluttering black shadows circling the two towers.

Peter grinned. His eyes lit up. "Bats!" he said.

"No!" I gasped. Peter knows I have a *thing* about bats. I hate them. I have nightmares about them. So of course he sees bats wherever we go — just to torture his big sister.

"They're birds," I said. "They've got to be some weird kind of bird."

"Definitely bats," Peter replied. He turned and gazed down the row of shops. "I don't see a movie theater, Abby. Hope Jonathan has an Internet connection. Or I'm gonna be totally bored."

"Hello there!" a voice called.

I turned around to see a woman crossing the platform toward us. She was very tall and had white-blond hair pulled tightly behind her head in a bun. Flashing blue eyes. Red lipsticked lips. She wore a long blue skirt that fluttered in the wind as she walked.

As she came closer, I saw the tattoo on her throat. A tattoo of a bluebird with its wings spread across her neck.

She had a blue canvas bag strapped to her back. And she carried a long loaf of bread under one arm.

She stopped and studied Peter and me. "Are you two okay?" she asked. She had a deep, velvety voice. "Are you all alone out here?"

"Our uncle was supposed to meet us," I said. "We took the train from Boston." I turned and pointed to the hill. "I think that might be his house up there."

The woman's mouth fell open. The loaf of bread dropped from under her arm. She caught it before it hit the pavement.

When she looked up, her eyes were filled with horror. "Oh, no!" she said. "You don't want to go up there! Listen to me. Go back where you came from. You *don't* want to go up to that house!"

3

A cold shiver ran down my back. Peter stepped close to me. He shoved his hands into his jeans pockets. He always does that when he's tense.

"Why?" I asked. "Why are you saying that?"

"What's wrong with Uncle Jonathan's house?" Peter demanded.

The woman gazed up at the big house on the hill. Then she slowly lowered her blue eyes to Peter and me. "I live up there, too," she said softly. "Very close by. Do you think I don't hear the strange *moans* at night?"

"Excuse me?" I said. "Moans?"

She frowned. "Think I don't know that something *horrible* goes on in that man's house?"

Was she *serious*?

No. She had to be mistaken. She had to be wrong. Granny Vee would *never* send us here if she thought it was dangerous.

I heard a pounding sound from down the road.

It took me a few seconds to realize it was hoofbeats.

I turned and saw a carriage — an old-fashioned carriage pulled by two tall black horses. The carriage came roaring toward the train station. Bouncing hard on the dirt parking lot, it raised clouds of dust behind it.

"Is that Uncle Jonathan?" Peter asked.

I watched the horses bobbing their heads as they thundered toward us. Then I turned back to the woman. "You were joking — right?" I asked.

"Sorry," she said. "I'm not sticking around. I don't ever want to see that man again."

She leaped off the platform. Her bread fell to the ground, but she didn't stop to pick it up. She just took off, running through the village. She didn't look back.

4

Peter and I huddled close together as the carriage squealed to a stop in front of us. The horses snorted and tossed their heads, breathing hard. Their backs were shiny with sweat.

As I gazed up at the old gray-haired driver, the carriage door swung open and a man lowered himself quickly to the ground. He was tall and handsome, with long, straight black hair parted in the middle and a black mustache.

A smile spread over his face as he came closer. His skin was pale, almost yellow, and tight against his cheekbones. His green eyes flashed. He gave us a quick wave with one hand.

He wore a loose-fitting gray suit over a white shirt, open at the neck. A black pipe poked out of his jacket pocket. His shiny black boots came up almost to his knees.

"Are you Abby and Peter?"

We nodded. "Uncle Jonathan?" I said.

The horses snorted behind him. They both pawed the gravel beside the platform.

"I thought I'd bring you to the house in style," Jonathan said. "Don't you love this wonderful antique carriage? It belonged to my great-grandfather."

"Awesome," Peter said. "It looks like it's from an old movie."

Jonathan smiled. When he smiled, his face crinkled into a thousand little lines. "I'll get your bags. Climb in."

A few minutes later, Peter and I sat side by side across from our uncle as the carriage bounced up the hill. The village disappeared beneath us as the horses pulled us toward the house.

"So sorry I was late," Jonathan said. "I wanted to make the house just right for you. I think you'll find it very exciting."

The carriage had a wonderful aroma of leather and wood. I gazed out the window at the passing trees. Then I raised my eyes to the roof of the house.

Those *were* bats circling the towers!

I could see them clearly now. But how could that be?

Bats aren't supposed to come out during the day.

The bats gave me another shiver. Like I said, bats have always freaked me out.

I suddenly remembered the woman with the bird tattoo. How horrified she looked when I told her we were going to this house.

Uncle Jonathan rolled his pipe between his fingers. He studied me. "How was your train ride?" he asked.

"Good," I said. "But there was a woman at the train station. When we were waiting for you . . ."

His dark eyebrows shot up. "A woman?"

"Yes. She got a little weird. She said she heard *moans* coming from your house at night."

Jonathan laughed. He had a dry, almost silent laugh. "Did she have a tattoo of a bird on her neck?"

"Yes," I said.

"That's Crazy Annie," he said. "She's always complaining about my dogs." He shook his head. "I hope she didn't scare you."

"No way," Peter said. He always acts like nothing scares him.

"She scared me a little," I said. "She told us not to go into your house. She told us to go back where we came from."

"Too late," Uncle Jonathan said. "We're here. You're my prisoners now."

5

Jonathan laughed. "Hey, I was joking. You'll get used to my weird sense of humor."

As I stepped inside the house, all thoughts of Crazy Annie vanished from my mind. My mouth dropped open as we made our way into the enormous front room.

"Have we gone back in time?" I cried. "It's like . . . we've stepped back into ancient Egypt!"

"Totally cool!" Peter declared.

My head was spinning. There was so much to see! The walls of the room looked just like pyramid bricks. They were covered with paintings of Egyptian cats, and pharaohs, and sphinxes, and all the stuff you see in museums.

Statues and strange animal sculptures filled the room. A small yellow-brick pyramid rose up beside the fireplace.

"What's that weird writing?" Peter asked Jonathan. He pointed to a large framed document on the wall. "Is that hieroglyphics?"

"Yes, it is," Jonathan answered. "The written language used by the ancient Egyptians. We have been able to translate some of it. But a lot of the symbols remain a mystery."

I stopped in front of a table that contained several tiny bird sculptures. They were dark blue and very shiny. I knew they were really old, but they looked new.

Jonathan saw me admiring the sculptures. "The Egyptians had a shade of blue that we cannot create today," he said. "Even with all our modern science we cannot match their glaze."

He sighed, and his eyes appeared to dim. "They were ahead of us in so many ways."

A faded orange-and-yellow painting of the sun hung on a wall over a tall stone sculpture. The sun had rays shooting from it and there were Egyptian symbols all around the borders.

"The Egyptians worshipped the sun god, Ra," Jonathan said. "That painting was made over two thousand years ago."

"Wow! This is amazing!" I exclaimed.

Jonathan smiled, the smile that crinkled up his face. "I spent a good part of my life in Egypt," he said. "As you can see, I'm a collector. I brought back many priceless treasures."

"Did you bring back a mummy?" Peter asked. "My friends and I are totally into mummies."

Jonathan smoothed his black mustache with his fingers. He narrowed his eyes at Peter. "You might see a mummy or two before your visit is over," he said.

"Cool!" Peter exclaimed. "Can I touch one?"

Before Jonathan could answer, a woman stepped into the room. She was short and plump with a round face and rosy cheeks. She had springy gray curls on her head. She wore a flowered apron over a long black housedress that hung down to her ankles.

Her glasses had slid halfway down her broad nose. She flashed us a toothy smile as she came nearer. "Faith be praised, Jonathan. Your house-guests have arrived at last!" she said. Her voice was very musical. She practically sang the words.

"Yes," Jonathan replied. "We've been waiting so eagerly, haven't we, Sonja?"

"Eagerly," Sonja repeated, grinning at me. "Yes, that's the truth of it."

Jonathan introduced us. Sonja was his house-keeper. "Sonja will see that you get everything you need," he told us.

"Have *you* seen the mummy?" Peter asked her.

The question startled Sonja. Her cheeks turned bright red. She squinted at Peter through her glasses. "Mummy? Upon my soul! No. Is there a mummy in this house?"

Jonathan shook his head. "Sonja is too busy to worry her head about mummies," he said. He turned to her. "Why don't you show Abby and Peter to their rooms?"

"Yes. You will like your rooms," she said.

She had her eyes locked on me. To my surprise, she stepped up close. Then she raised her chubby fingers — and ran them through my hair.

"What beautiful long black hair," she sang. "Upon my mother's heart. Beautiful, beautiful."

What is up with her? I wondered. *How totally weird to run your hands through a stranger's hair.*

"See you at dinner," Jonathan said, waving at us with the pipe in his hand. Was I imagining it? Or was he staring at my hair, too?

Sonja led the way up a wide stone stairway. Enormous tapestries with ancient Egyptian symbols hung on the walls.

"It's like living in a museum," Peter whispered.

Sonja led us down a long, dark hall. Old-fashioned torches poked out from the walls, making the shadows flicker and dance. The floor was marble, and our footsteps echoed as we walked.

Sonja stopped suddenly and pointed to a dark wooden door at the end of the hall. "You will enjoy exploring your uncle's house," she said. "But never open that door."

She lowered her voice to a whisper. "Those are Dr. Jonathan's private quarters. Do not go there unless he invites you."

We turned and started down another dimly lit hallway. But I stopped when I thought I heard sounds from the other side of that door.

Moans? Low groans?

The sounds sent a chill down the back of my neck. And the woman at the train station flashed into my mind.

Jonathan called her Crazy Annie.

But was she telling the *truth* about this place?

My room was big and bright and totally weird. It had heavy purple drapes over the windows and a crystal chandelier that threw a sparkly light over everything.

I gazed at the canopy bed with its curtains flowing down the sides. The curtains and bedspread were purple to match the drapes. I'd never slept in a canopy bed. I knew I'd feel like a princess in a movie!

This room, too, was filled with ancient Egyptian objects. I walked around picking up clay vases and jars, little pipes, and bird sculptures. Even the pale wallpaper had rows of ancient Egyptians all over it, standing in their funny sideways pose.

Are all the rooms in this house decorated like ancient Egypt? I wondered. *Uncle Jonathan must be totally* obsessed*!*

I lugged my suitcase onto the bed and opened it. It would be easy to unpack. The closet in this

22

room was bigger than my whole bedroom at Granny Vee's!

I bent down and pulled a stack of T-shirts from the suitcase. And *screamed* when a cold blast shocked the back of my neck!

My breath caught in my throat.

I spun around.

"Peter!" I screamed. "No fair!"

He aimed his blaster and sent a spray of water over the front of my jeans.

"No fair! I don't have my blaster!" I wailed.

I ducked, and the next stream of water sailed over my head.

Peter laughed. "You lose, Abby!"

"That's the only way you can win," I said, wiping the back of my neck with one hand. "Shoot an unarmed person."

I rummaged in my suitcase till I found the water blaster at the bottom. I tugged it out and pointed it at my brother's face. I pulled the trigger.

He ducked, then dropped to the floor.

It was my turn to laugh. "It's not loaded, you idiot. Think I'd put a loaded water gun in my suitcase?"

He climbed to his feet. "We can have awesome water battles in this place!"

"Maybe," I said. "Uncle Jonathan might not like it — with all these valuable museum objects everywhere."

I took out my toiletry bag and carried it to the bathroom. "Did you unpack?" I called to Peter.

"Kinda," he replied.

"What do you mean *kinda?*"

He shrugged. "I took some stuff out. You know." He picked up my backpack and began pawing through it.

I grabbed it away from him. "What's your problem, Peter?"

"Looking for your phone," he said. "Can we call Granny Vee?"

His voice came out high and shrill. He suddenly sounded like such a little boy.

I could see the worry on his face. I had been thinking about Granny Vee, too.

"Sure," I said. I pulled my cell from the bag and clicked it on. "Hey — good news. Three bars," I said. "It works here."

I punched in Granny Vee's number, and she picked up after the third ring. "Granny Vee — it's me!" I said. "Peter and I are here with Uncle Jonathan, and everything is fine."

"I'm so glad you called," she said. She coughed and cleared her throat. Her voice sounded hoarse.

"Granny Vee, how are you feeling?" I asked.

"P-pretty good," she answered. "I get tired so easily, but —" She stopped.

"When do you go in for the tests?" I asked.

"Tomorrow," she replied. "But I don't want you

two to worry. I want you to enjoy your stay with Jonathan. He's such an interesting man. And he was so eager to have you."

"He sure loves ancient Egypt," I said.

"Really?" she replied. She sounded surprised.

Peter interrupted. "Ask her if we can come home next week."

"No, I won't," I whispered. "Granny Vee said we'll stay here for two weeks."

"Don't worry about me," Granny Vee said, coughing some more. "I'll be fine."

"We'll call you tomorrow," I said.

I clicked off. "She sounds kind of weak," I told Peter. "She keeps saying she'll be fine. I hope she's telling the truth."

"Me, too," Peter murmured.

I yawned. I suddenly felt really tired. Guess it was the long train ride.

I took my brother by the shoulders and pushed him to the door. "Peter, go unpack," I said. "Don't leave all your stuff in the suitcase."

He groaned. "Bor-ring!" He raised his water blaster and pointed it at me. "Squirt, squirt," he said. Then he stomped on my foot and ran off.

Is he a total *jerk or just a jerk?* I asked myself.

By the time I finished unpacking, I was yawning my head off. I couldn't keep my eyes open.

The quilted bedspread on the canopy bed looked soft and inviting. I decided to take a short nap.

I pulled off my shoes and climbed on top of the spread. *Mmmmmm.* So soft. I sank into it. I stretched my arms, rubbing them against the velvety smoothness.

I shut my eyes.

And drifted off to sleep almost instantly. I felt so snug and comfortable, as if I were floating on air.

I don't know how long I slept. I blinked my eyes open — half awake — and saw something.

A dark creature. It slithered silently into my room.

First, I saw its shadow on the wall. And then I saw it leap.

It sprang onto the bed — onto my chest! And before I could move or scream, it reached out and started to *choke* me!

7

I opened my mouth in a frightened scream.

I heard footsteps.

Someone came bursting through the bedroom door.

Sonja ran up to my bed — and pulled the creature off my chest.

I stared up at it as it squirmed in her hands.

A black cat. A very big black cat with olivegreen eyes.

Gasping for breath, my heart thudding, I sat up. I could still feel the dry paws on my throat.

Sonja held the cat tightly around its middle.

The cat was black except for a tiny V of white on her chest. Her olive eyes were locked on mine. It creeped me out. It was almost a human stare.

"I see you've met Cleopatra," Sonja said.

"Huh? Cleopatra?" I choked out.

"By my faith, I'm sorry she scared you," Sonja said. "She doesn't take to visitors."

I blinked. "That's the biggest cat I ever saw!" I said. She was long and lean. She had to be as big as Granny Vee's old cocker spaniel!

"She comes from a long, long line of Egyptian cats," Sonja said.

She rubbed Cleopatra's belly. The cat stopped struggling. It went limp. But kept its intense stare on me.

I had the weird feeling it was trying to communicate, trying to tell me something.

But — what?

"An ancient breed," Sonja said. "Your Uncle Jonathan brought her back with him from Cairo."

"How long ago?" I asked. "How old is she?"

Sonja shrugged. "The cat is not young. She is set in her ways. She doesn't like change."

"I . . . I don't think she likes *me*!" I said.

Sonja shrugged again. She set Cleopatra down on the floor.

The cat gave me one last long look. A pink triangular tongue darted out, and she licked her lips from side to side. Then, with her slender tail raised, she scampered silently out the door.

I lowered my feet to the floor. My stomach growled. "Is it almost dinnertime?" I asked.

Sonja didn't answer. She was eyeing my hair again.

I realized it must be a tangled mess. I hadn't brushed it since we arrived.

"Such beautiful hair," she said. Her round cheeks turned red. She smiled as she reached out. And she smoothed my hair down against my head.

I felt a shiver. *Creepy*, I thought.

"Such beautiful hair," Sonja whispered. "By my soul, it will not go to waste."

"*Excuse* me?" I said. "*What* did you say?"

But she turned and hurried from the room.

8

"So there I was in Egypt, floating up the Nile river for the first time in my life," Uncle Jonathan said at dinner. "One of the longest, most famous rivers in the world. I was in a flatboat, heading south from Cairo."

Peter set down his chicken leg. "Were you afraid?" he asked.

Jonathan stared across the table at him. "What a strange question," he said. "No, I was excited. *Thrilled*. To be traveling on the same river that the pharaohs sailed."

Peter thought for a moment. "But weren't you afraid of the mummies?" he asked.

Jonathan wiped gravy off his mustache. He smiled. "Peter, you don't see mummies everywhere you look in Egypt," he said. "Most of them are in museums. Or else they are buried deep in their tombs."

"Well, are you going to show us a mummy?" Peter asked.

Jonathan and I laughed. "Peter, you're *obsessed*!" I cried. "You have mummies on the brain!"

"So what?" He stuck out his tongue at me.

"Maybe after dinner," Jonathan said. "Finish your chicken. And let me finish my story."

"Fried chicken and mashed potatoes are my favorites," I said.

"It was a sunny day," Jonathan continued. "I could see silvery fish swimming in the river. Whole schools of them. Well... I wasn't very smart. I told you it was my first trip. I leaned over the side of the flatboat to see the fish better — and *splash* — I fell into the river!"

"Whoa!" I cried. "Was it deep?"

He nodded. "Pretty deep. I'm not a great swimmer. And the boat was moving faster than I'd thought. I sputtered and thrashed, and the boat was sailing away from me."

"No one saw you?" Peter asked.

"I guess not," Jonathan answered. "I started swimming after the boat as fast as I could. But then I felt these *things* swim up my pants legs. And I knew I was in trouble."

I swallowed. "What were they?"

"I'm not sure," Jonathan replied. "Some kind of vicious eels, I guess. They swam right up my pants, twined around my legs, and bit off big hunks of my skin."

31

"And what happened?" Peter asked.

Jonathan shook his head sadly. "They chewed off my legs, and I died."

Peter and I stared at him. The big dining room was silent.

Then Jonathan burst out laughing. "Sorry," he said. "People tell me I have a sick sense of humor."

Then Peter and I started to laugh. We thought Jonathan was telling us a true story. We didn't know he liked to joke so much.

After dinner, Sonja brought us big slices of apple pie with vanilla ice cream. It was an awesome dinner. I think Jonathan was trying to make us feel at home.

But I could see Peter was starting to get fidgety. He never likes to sit still for more than ten minutes. At home, he laps up his food like a dog in five seconds, jumps up from the table, and asks Granny Vee to be excused.

Jonathan ate the last bite of pie and set down his fork. He smiled at Peter. "Okay, okay," he said. "I know what you're thinking. Follow me."

Peter jumped up excitedly. "You're going to show us a mummy?"

"Just follow me," Jonathan said. He put his hands on Peter's shoulders and guided him out of the dining room. "Peter, where did you get your interest in mummies?" he asked.

"From movies," Peter said. "I like it when they come to life and stagger around, strangling people."

Jonathan laughed. "I like those movies, too. But sometimes I wish they were more realistic. You know, the *real* stories are even scarier."

He led us down a long, curving hallway. Tall oil portraits of old-fashioned people hung on the walls. They all looked very grim, as if they had just heard some bad news. Some of them looked a lot like Jonathan. I guessed they were his ancestors. And mine, too.

I glimpsed a library filled with books from floor to ceiling. Another room had a pool table and a dark wooden bar. We passed a study with a wide desk cluttered with papers and files. The doors to several rooms were closed.

"I'm taking you to the temple." Jonathan's voice echoed as we made our way down a steep flight of stairs. "It's a perfect re-creation of an ancient one in Egypt. It took me three years to build it in my house."

"Cool," Peter muttered.

We went down another flight of stairs. The air grew hot and thick. The back of my neck prickled with sweat.

We turned a corner and followed Jonathan down another hall. "This house is humongous," I said. "A person could get lost here!"

"You're right," Jonathan said. "Once, I got lost here for two years!"

This time, Peter and I laughed. We were getting used to his sense of humor.

He led us up to tall double doors. The doors were guarded by two stone statues on pedestals. The statues had to be ten feet tall! They looked like giant open-mouthed cats, only fierce. Fiery torches jutted out from the wall above them.

Jonathan pulled open the heavy doors. "This is the temple," he said in a whisper.

We stepped into the huge room. Our footsteps echoed on the stone floor. The ceiling was high above our heads. The room was dark except for a blazing fire dancing high in a wide brick fireplace.

I waited for my eyes to adjust to the dim light. And then, in front of the fire, I saw a small rectangle. A mummy case. Standing on its end.

Peter was so excited, he leaped into the air. I could feel my heart start to race.

We followed Jonathan up to the case. To my surprise, it was exactly my height.

Jonathan rested his hand on its top. "It's Ka-Ran-Tut," he whispered. "The Boy Pharaoh."

The firelight cast strange shadows over Jonathan as he bent to open the lid. He seemed to fade in and out of view. The logs cracked loudly, and bright red embers flew out from the fireplace.

The lid slid open quickly. I gasped as I saw the mummy. So short! So tiny and frail.

"He was your age, Peter," Jonathan said. He stepped back so we could see the mummy clearly.

My breath caught in my throat. His head looked so delicate. The ragged wrappings were torn and stained. Some of them had unraveled off his skinny arms, which were crossed in front of him. His feet had turned black.

"Come closer," Jonathan said, waving his arms. "You can see better."

Peter's mouth hung open. His eyes were bulging.

"He was your age," Jonathan repeated, "but he ruled Egypt when he was four years old. By the time he was seven, he was responsible for the deaths of nearly two thousand people."

"Wow," Peter muttered. "He was a bad kid, huh?"

"You could say that," Jonathan replied.

"I . . . I can't believe this *thing* was once a real, live boy," I said. I shook my head. "I know I'm gonna have nightmares tonight!"

I leaned closer. I wondered if I could see his eyes and mouth under the wrappings.

I brought my face right up to the mummy's. And then I *gasped* as I heard its dry whisper:

"Who's your mummy?"

With a short cry, I staggered back. I nearly fell.

I heard Peter's loud laugh. "Scared you!" he cried. He gave me a shove and laughed some more.

"Did NOT!" I shouted. "I *knew* it was you!"

Peter stuck his grinning face up to mine. "If you knew it was me, why did you scream? And why did you jump back like that?"

"Just wanted to give you a thrill," I said. I shoved him back.

"Please. Remember this is a temple," Jonathan said. He carefully slid shut the cover of the mummy case.

"Do you have any more mummies?" Peter asked him. "Any big ones?"

Jonathan didn't answer. He made sure the mummy's lid was closed tight. Then he brushed some dust off the front.

"You'll have plenty of time to explore my house," he said finally. His eyes sparkled in the dancing firelight. "Who *knows* what amazing things you will find?"

Peter didn't want to go to sleep. He was too wired from his first view of a real mummy. He danced around my room, talking a mile a minute. Almost climbing the walls. The way he gets when he eats too much chocolate.

Finally, I had to take him by the hands and drag him down the hall to his room.

Later, I thought about calling Granny Vee. But it was too late. She was probably asleep.

I sank into the big bed and pulled the silky bedspread up to my chin. When I shut my eyes, I pictured the frail little mummy.

Was there really a boy inside all that gauze and tar? Did he really have two thousand people killed by the time he was seven?

The thought gave me a chill. I pulled the covers up even higher.

I was nearly asleep when I heard the sounds. Soft voices, but close by.

I jerked myself up, totally alert. And listened.

Low moans. Groans. Like someone in pain.

Someone nearby. Moaning in pain. Over and over.

Just as Crazy Annie had warned!

Were the sounds coming from the next room?

I lowered my feet to the carpet. I realized I was trembling all over.

"Got to find Uncle Jonathan," I murmured.

I pushed the bedspread away and stood up. I started to the door but stopped in the middle of the room.

I felt a cold wind brush my back. And heard a cracking noise outside.

I froze. It took me a few seconds to realize I was listening to the brittle snap of wings.

Bat wings!

I spun around. The bedroom window was open. The long drapes billowed in the gusting wind.

I pictured the bats again, circling low around the towers of the house.

And now they were *right outside my room*!

I lurched to the window. I started to tug it down — when I heard a loud squeal.

And a huge bat — eyes glowing bright red — flew screeching into my room.

10

"Noooooo!"

I let out a scream and jumped back from the window.

Screeching louder, the bat swooped past my face. I felt its wings brush my cheek.

It flew around me in a wild circle, flapping hard. The red eyes glowed as if on fire. And its shrill whistle rang in my ears.

I raised both hands. Tried to slap it away.

Again, I felt the brush of its dry wings against my skin. I tried to bury my face in my hands. I could feel the bursts of air from its body as it whipped around me.

It made one more circle — then dove out the window.

I groaned with relief. Staggered forward — and slammed the window shut.

Trembling from head to foot, I struggled to slow my frantic breathing.

I gripped the sides of the window as if holding

on for dear life. Pressing my hot forehead against the cool glass, I peered out into the night.

I could see the pointed roof of the other tower, lighted by a bright half moon. A dozen bats swooped and soared, flapping in wide circles around the tower.

My breath caught in my throat as I watched them dive low, then swoop back up, then dive down again.

Something had them stirred up.

I lowered my gaze to the lawn — and pulled my face back from the window with a gasp.

A man stood on the grass with his arms raised, trying to fight off the bats.

I took a deep breath and returned to the window. I could see him clearly in the moonlight. He was tall and broad. Powerful looking. He cast a long shadow on the grass in front of him.

An evil-looking man, wearing a long, baggy black overcoat.

He raised his face to my window. *Did he see me?*

I tried to hide behind the heavy drape while still staring down at him. In the pale yellow light, I saw a long scar across his bald head. His mouth set in a tight, angry scowl.

Who was he? What did he want?

He swung his big hands in front of him, waving off the swooping bats. And took a few lumbering steps across the grass toward the house.

I heard the flap of wings. And let out a cry as a dozen screeching bats went on the attack. They plunged past my window and dove at the man, flapping hard, red eyes glaring furiously.

The big man tried to duck and dodge. But there were too many bats to slap away.

He began swinging his arms wildly. I could hear his cries as the bats tore at his coat, bounced off his chest.

Bats clung to his shoulders and scratched at his throat. A flapping bat sank its claws into the man's bald head, wailing like a siren.

The man staggered back. He fell — and the bats followed him down.

More bats dove onto his chest as he struggled to scramble to his feet. Bats scratched their claws across his face. Flapping wings covered his head.

"This is HORRIBLE!" I screamed. "They're tearing him to *pieces*!"

11

I turned away. I couldn't bear to watch.

Didn't Uncle Jonathan hear the man's screams?

Gripping the drape in my fists, I leaned to the window. And saw the man running away. He'd left his overcoat behind on the grass, like a present to the bats. He was racing full speed down the hill, waving his arms wildly as he ran.

The bats swooped high above his head and circled him, following him down the hill. They didn't dive or attack. It was like they just wanted to make sure he didn't come back.

I let go of the drape. My hands were ice-cold. My teeth were chattering.

I straightened my nightshirt and ran out into the dimly lit hall. "Uncle Jonathan?" I screamed. "Uncle Jonathan?"

I gazed up and down the hall. Where was his bedroom?

After a few seconds, I heard the clumping sound

of running footsteps. Sonja came trotting around a corner, fastening her robe as she ran.

"Sonja! A man! A man outside!" I choked out.

She wrapped me in a hug. Her cheeks were hot. She smelled of a flowery perfume.

"Are you okay? Oh, my soul — you're shivering. Are you okay?" She kept repeating the words.

"Yes. B-but the man —" I stammered. "I saw him out my window. It was horrible! The bats —"

"You weren't harmed?" She petted my hair. "*Shhhhh. Shhhhh.* Take a deep breath. I'll say a little prayer of thanks."

"Sonja —" I was starting to calm down. But I couldn't get the picture out of my mind of those bats biting and scratching and screeching. "The bats attacked the man. I watched —"

She raised a finger to her lips. "Sometimes strangers come wandering up the hill," she said in a whisper. "The bats like to protect the house. Upon my faith, child, they always chase the intruders away."

"But it was so frightening," I said. "The way the bats swooped all over him —"

Her dark eyes locked on mine. "The man learned a lesson tonight. He will know not to return," she whispered.

She wrapped a heavy arm around my shoulders. And led me back to my room. "Climb into your warm bed," she said. "I'll tuck you in."

She smoothed my hair as I climbed under the bedspread. "Sleep tight, now," she whispered. "By my heart, you will not be harmed here." She tugged the spread under my chin.

I watched her tiptoe from the room. I could still smell her strong, flowery perfume.

My head sank into the soft pillow. I shut my eyes, but I knew it would take a long time to fall asleep.

My heart was racing in my chest. And I could still hear the flapping of bat wings outside the window.

As the bat noises finally faded, another sound rose up nearby. Once again, I heard the low moans and groans. So close . . . On the other side of the wall!

The eerie, frightening moans rising and falling.

Was I imagining it? Was I hearing wrong?

For a moment, I thought I heard words. A low chant rising from the sad moans. The same words repeated over and over:

"I want to die. . . . I want to die. . . . I want to die. . . ."

12

The next morning, I hurried down to the kitchen in my nightshirt. My hair was a tangled mess, but I didn't care. I was eager to ask Jonathan about the bats and the evil-looking man and the groans and moans — and *everything*!

Peter already sat at the breakfast table, spooning up a big bowl of cereal. He had milk all over his chin. He gave me a wide, openmouthed grin so I could see the chewed-up mush in his mouth.

Jonathan had both hands wrapped around a tall white mug of coffee. He smiled when he saw me enter the kitchen and motioned to the empty chair opposite him.

"Peter, did you sleep?" I asked.

He nodded.

"Didn't you hear the bats or the man screaming or anything?"

He shook his head and kept shoving cereal into his mouth. "You're crazy," he said, dribbling milk over his chin, back into the bowl.

"No, she isn't," Jonathan interrupted. He turned to me. "Abby, I'm so sorry about last night. Sonja told me everything, and I really do apologize. Your first night here, and it turned into something of a nightmare."

"It was totally frightening," I said. "I saw the bats and —"

Jonathan reached across the table and patted my hand. "I'm so sorry. Let me explain. I keep a bat cave under the house. The bat is one of the creatures that I study."

Sonja set a plate of scrambled eggs and bacon in front of me. I thanked her, but I wasn't ready to eat breakfast. I still had a lot of questions for Uncle Jonathan.

"There was a man on the lawn —" I started.

Jonathan nodded. "As you saw, my house *is* a target for thieves," he said. "It's only natural. I have so many valuable objects."

He took another long drink of coffee. Then he wiped his mustache with his napkin. "Sonja told me you were frightened by that intruder last night," he said. "I don't want you to worry, Abby. This house is safe from anyone who tries to get in."

"Your eggs are getting cold," Sonja said, standing at the kitchen door.

I picked up my fork and began to eat. I was starting to feel better. I started to ask my next question, but Peter interrupted me.

"Can we go into the village?" he asked Jonathan. "My iPod is broken. I think I need a new one."

Jonathan frowned at Peter. "I don't think we can go into town today," he said. "My work is keeping me much too busy. Besides, you won't find a store in this tiny village that sells any kind of electronics. I have to buy everything I need by mail."

"Snail mail?" Peter said. "That's lame. You mean you don't have an Internet hookup here?"

Jonathan started to respond. But the phone rang. He left the room to answer it.

"Peter, you have to be a better guest," I whispered. "It's not very nice to tell Jonathan that the way he does things is *lame*."

"Not what I meant," Peter mumbled. He shot a spoonful of his cereal milk across the table at me. It dripped down the front of my nightshirt.

"Thanks a lot," I said. "How did you get to be such a pain?"

"I learned everything I know from my big sister," he said.

Funny dude.

I finished breakfast and hurried up the stairs to my room. Bright sunlight poured through the window. The sky was clear and blue.

I changed into jeans and a bright yellow tank top. Then I sat down at the dressing table to brush my hair.

47

Talk about luxury! Can you imagine having your own dressing table? It was all gold and marble. With a soft little bench in front of it and a tall mirror in the back.

I raised the brush to my hair, stroked it through once . . . twice . . .

Something felt wrong.

My hair gets pretty tangled at night. But it doesn't take long to fix it.

But this morning, something was definitely strange.

I leaned forward and brought my face close to the mirror. I turned my head to see the side.

No.

No.

Impossible.

A chunk of my hair had been cut off.

I didn't want to believe it. I raised some of my hair in one hand and brought it close to the mirror. I squinted hard at it.

But no amount of wishing would bring it back. I had to face the truth. A big chunk of hair. Gone.

Who would *do* that to me?

I let the hairbrush fall to my lap. Stunned, I stared at myself in the mirror. Gazed into the sunlight reflected in the glass. And tried to think clearly.

I heard soft footsteps behind me.

Before I could turn around, I was stabbed in the back.

I let out a scream. Felt the prickle of pain spread.

I spun around — and shook Cleopatra off me. She tumbled to the floor. Landed on her back. But instantly stood up. And stared at me with those bright olive eyes.

"Ow!" I said, trying to rub my back. But I couldn't reach the spot that hurt. "You evil cat! Can't you just stay off me?"

And then I saw my water blaster on the side of the dressing table. And remembered I'd filled it full last night.

"Aha! Revenge is mine!" I cried.

I grabbed up the blaster, spun it around — and gave the black cat a good soaking from head to foot.

I laughed. And waited for Cleopatra to turn and run.

But no.

No.

The cat didn't move.

The color faded from her eyes. Her ears drooped. Her head appeared to sag.

As I stared in horror, pieces of the cat dropped to the floor. The tail crumbled to dust. The eyes rolled out. The head crumpled and fell off the body.

In seconds, I was gaping at a pile of black powder. The cat had *disintegrated* into a dry mound of ashes at my feet.

13

I pressed my hands to my face and let out a cry. As I looked at the dark ashes, wave after wave of panic swept over me.

My stomach lurched. I shut my eyes and spun away from it.

"This is wrong. This is horribly WRONG!" I cried in a trembling voice.

I sucked in a deep breath — and took off. "Peter! Hey, Peter!" I shouted as I hurtled down the long, dimly lit hall.

My shoes thudded on the hard floor. I stopped at Peter's open doorway. "We've got to get OUT of here!" I screamed.

He was sprawled on his bed, reading a manga book. His open laptop was on the floor beside the bed. There were clothes strewn everywhere.

"Excuse me?" He glanced up from his comic. "What's your problem, Abby?"

"We — we've got to get *out* of this house!" I cried breathlessly. "We've got to find Uncle

Jonathan. Let's tell him Granny Vee called, and she needs us back."

Peter sat up, yawning. "You're joking, right?"

I ran into the room, grabbed him by the arm, and pulled him to his feet. "Listen to me. Something is very wrong here," I said. "The cat . . . Cleopatra . . ."

"What a totally creepy cat," Peter said.

"Not anymore," I said. I handed him his sneakers. "I squirted her with my water blaster — and she FELL APART! I mean, she totally FELL TO PIECES!"

His eyes went wide. "You mean you *killed* her?"

"I just squirted her, and she crumbled to *ashes*!" I said. "Hurry. Put on your shoes. We can't stay here."

He finally believed me. He pulled on his sneakers and followed me into the hall. "How are we going to get away?" he asked.

"I think the train comes every day," I said. "We'll just tell Jonathan we're needed back home. And he'll drive us to the train station."

"But . . . shouldn't we call Granny Vee?" Peter asked in a tiny voice.

"Later," I said. "First, let's get out of this house!"

We took the stairs two at a time. We searched the front rooms, the den, the kitchen, and dining room. No sign of Jonathan or Sonja.

"Uncle Jonathan?" Peter cupped his hands around his mouth and shouted his name. "Where are you?"

Peter's voice echoed down the hall. But no reply.

"Let's try his bedroom," I said. We scrambled back up the stairs, running side by side. Down the long hall.

His bedroom door was open just a crack. "Uncle Jonathan? Are you in there?" I called.

No answer.

"Uncle Jonathan?"

I pushed open the door. The wind was blowing the brown curtains at the window. He had draped a black jacket over a tall stone sculpture of a sphinx. The bed was unmade. A blanket lay crumpled on the floor.

"He's not here," Peter muttered.

Seconds later, we found ourselves at the dark wooden door at the end of the hall. Jonathan's private quarters.

I reached my hand up to knock, but Peter pulled it down. "We're not allowed to go in there, remember?"

"This is an emergency," I said.

I pounded on the door with my fist.

No answer.

I grabbed the doorknob, turned it, and pushed the door open. I poked my head in. A strong odor greeted my nose.

"Smells like a doctor's office," Peter whispered.

We stepped into a huge room with high ceilings and dark red wallpaper. Bright sunlight poured in through a row of tall windows.

I waited for my eyes to adjust to the bright light. And then I gasped. "Are these all mummy cases?"

Peter grabbed my hand. "This is awesome!" he whispered. "There must be *dozens* of them. Think there's a mummy in every case?"

I stared at the three long rows of cases all lined up perfectly. They filled the room.

"I . . . I don't know," I murmured. "This is totally freaking me out."

I took a step — and then stopped.

A low moan rose up from the nearest mummy case.

I heard a sigh. Another moan. A long groan.

As if the mummies were ALIVE!

My breath caught in my throat. My chest felt tight, as if I were about to *explode* from fright.

Last night, I heard the moans through my bedroom wall. I never dreamed they were coming from living mummies. Or . . . was someone — or something — *else* living in these coffinlike cases?

I turned to leave. I *had* to get out of there.

But Peter spun me around. "Look, Abby." He pointed.

A door across the room, slightly open.

Was Uncle Jonathan back there?

Questions flashed in my mind: *What kind of work did he do in here? Why did he have these mummies hidden away?*

I didn't want to know the answers. I just wanted to get *out* of the house.

Peter and I crept past the rows of mummy cases. The moans and groans rose up on both sides of us. But I kept my eyes on the door and didn't turn my head. I didn't want to see them.

We stepped up to the door and peered inside. The room was brightly lit. It looked sparkling clean, with white walls and a white ceiling.

I saw electronic equipment lined up against the back wall. Metal tables. Oxygen tanks. It looked kind of like a hospital operating room.

I jerked my head back when I saw Jonathan.

He stood behind a long metal table. He was leaning over a mummy.

The mummy was on its back. Its arms hung over the sides of the table.

Carefully, I peeked back into the room. Jonathan had his head down. He didn't see Peter and me.

I didn't breathe. I didn't move. I stared in disbelief at my uncle as he leaned over the mummy. His eyes were wild. His face was red with excitement.

He tugged up his shirtsleeves. Shook his hands as if shaking off water.

He slowly, carefully began to unwrap the ancient bandages.

Then he *dug* his hands into the mummy's belly.

He dug both hands in deep — and pulled out a glistening dark purple organ. A kidney? A liver?

"Ohhhh, sick!" I moaned.

And then I watched him raise the disgusting wet mummy guts to his mouth — and start to *eat* them!

14

My stomach heaved. My throat tightened. I started to gag.

How could he eat mummy guts? How could there be guts inside the mummy?

I stumbled back from the door and almost knocked Peter over. I shut my eyes but I could still see him . . . Uncle Jonathan shoving the raw purple guts into his mouth . . . liquid running down his chin . . . chewing it, chewing the ancient mummy guts so hungrily . . . his eyes wild, rolling around in his excited face.

"Sick," Peter muttered, holding his stomach. He let out a groan. "I think I'm going to be sick. Really."

"No time for that," I whispered. "We have to get out of here — now! He's *crazy*! He's totally nuts! Peter — hurry. We have to get help!"

We turned and ran. Our footsteps thudded loudly through the big room of mummies.

The mummies moaned as we ran between them toward the door. And again, I thought I heard more than one of them murmur, *"Please — let me die! Let me die!"*

We burst through the door and ran down the long hall. My heart was pounding so hard, I could barely breathe.

Did Jonathan hear us? Was he coming after us?

I glanced back. No. No sign of him.

Peter and I ran into my bedroom. I closed the door behind us.

"Don't panic. Don't panic," I said breathlessly. I guess I was trying to calm myself down. Because I was totally freaking out. I'd never been so frightened in my life.

"How could he eat that stuff?" Peter asked in a tiny voice. His face was green. He held his stomach again. "It . . . it must taste so rotten. He . . . he was eating a DEAD PERSON!"

I felt sick, too. I raised a hand. "Stop," I said. "Stop thinking about it."

He dropped onto the edge of my bed. He shook his head. "What are we going to do? He's a maniac. We can't stay here."

My head was spinning. *Don't panic. Abby, don't panic*, I told myself again.

I grabbed my cell phone off the bed table. "I'll call 911," I said. "The village police. They *have* to have police in the village — right?"

I flipped open the phone and started to punch in the number.

Then I uttered a startled cry. "The battery! Peter — look!"

I held up the phone. "The battery is *gone*! Someone stole the battery from my phone!"

Peter's mouth dropped open. "He . . . he doesn't want us to call anyone," he stammered.

I grabbed my jacket. Then I tugged Peter to his feet. "Come on. Get your coat. We're outta here."

He held back. "But — where can we go?"

"To the village," I said. "Maybe we can find the police station. Or maybe there will be a train, and we can get out of here."

I poked my head out into the hall. Empty. No sign of Jonathan or Sonja. "Let's go!"

We hurried to Peter's room. He grabbed his hoodie and slipped it on. Then we made our way down the stairs.

"The kitchen phone!" I said, pointing to the black phone on the wall. I grabbed the receiver off the hook and raised it to my ear.

Silent.

Dead.

I pulled Peter toward the front door. "We have no choice. We can make it down the hill. I know we can. It's only a couple of miles to the village."

We stepped outside, into a gray, dark day. Clouds had covered the sun.

I felt a cold drizzle on my head and shoulders. A thick fog had swept over the hill. The fog was so thick, I couldn't see the village down below.

I shivered and zipped my jacket to the top. A cold raindrop landed on my nose. I wiped it away. The swirling fog felt icy and damp.

"I can't see a thing," Peter said. "This fog is like smoke."

"That's good," I said. "If Jonathan comes after us, he won't see us. It'll be easy to hide."

Staying close together, we found the road that curved down the steep hill. Peter pulled the hood over his head. We started walking, fast, almost jogging.

But the old road was pitted with holes and deep ruts. I tripped and stumbled to the ground. Peter helped pull me up. My knee throbbed with pain, but I forced myself to keep moving fast.

I kept glancing back to see if Jonathan was following us. But I couldn't see a thing in the heavy fog.

The fog brightened, grew so bright I had to squint. Then it swirled and grew dark again, until it felt as if we had gone from day to night.

Suddenly, Peter stopped. He tilted his head. "What's that sound?"

A few seconds later, I heard it, too. A helicopter flying above us?

I squinted into the dark fog blanket. I heard a shrill, chittering sound. And then I saw them.

Bats.

Like black shadows in the fog. Darting low over our heads, then swooping back up, disappearing in the layers of mist.

"The bats are following us!" Peter cried.

I ducked as a shrieking bat flapped right over my head. I could feel the wind off its wings, and then it vanished into the fog.

The road curved around a thicket of scraggly pine bushes. Peter and I made the turn. I had my hands over my head, trying to shield myself from the screeching bats. My legs ached from the long downhill trek.

And I kept turning back, watching the road behind us. Listening for Jonathan's car. Once he discovered we were gone, I knew he'd come after us.

It seemed to take hours. The bats screeched and chattered and swooped. They followed us all the way down the hill.

The trees gave way to tall grass and weeds. And the fog finally lifted as we neared the village of Cranford.

Peter and I trotted down the center of Main Street, past the small shops and houses. A black cat stared at us through a store window, and I thought of Cleopatra.

In my mind, I saw it all once again. Saw the cat's look of surprise when I squirted it with water. Saw the cat fall to pieces . . . to powder. A shudder ran down my body.

We stopped across from the little train station. No one on the platform. No one in the street.

"Where is everyone?" Peter asked. "Someone has to help us. I —"

We both saw the man at the same time. He came around the corner of the train station. His eyes went wide when he saw us.

I recognized him — and gasped.

The evil-looking bald man with the scar on his forehead. The intruder from last night.

"*There* you are!" he growled.

He stretched his arms out wide as if he was ready to capture us. And he came rushing toward us!

15

"Nooooo!"

A scream burst from my throat.

Peter and I turned and took off running across the street. We ducked into a narrow alley between a barbershop and a dry cleaners.

The alley was dark and cold. Our footsteps thudded on the hard pavement.

We reached the end of the alley and ran into a small park.

"Come back here!" the big man bellowed. His deep voice echoed off the alley walls. He wasn't far behind.

We ran over the wet grass of the park and ducked behind a row of low evergreen shrubs.

The man saw us. He picked up speed, his big legs churning. His face was bright red. His eyes were wild and desperate.

Peter glanced around frantically. How could we escape him?

No place to hide. No place.

I darted away from the shrubs and ran back to the narrow alley. Peter was close behind me. I could hear his wheezing breath. We couldn't run much longer.

A few seconds later, we found ourselves back on Main Street, in front of the train station.

Now what?

I glanced up and down the street. No one around. No one to help us.

I was so desperate to find someone, I didn't see the black car pull up. It stopped beside us, and the driver's window slid down.

"Get in!" a voice called. "Hurry!"

I squinted into the car. It was Crazy Annie! She waved to us frantically.

In the alley, I saw the big man lumbering toward us. He was waving, too. Waving both arms as he ran.

"Get in!" Annie cried. "Hurry! I warned you! Get in! I'll take you away from that madman!"

I held back. Did Jonathan tell the truth? Was Annie really crazy?

If so, we shouldn't get in the car with her.

But the big man with the scar was just *too scary*.

I pulled open the back door of the car and pushed Peter inside. Then I dove onto the seat. My legs were still dangling out of the car when Annie floored the gas pedal and the car roared forward.

The big man leaped in front of the car to stop us.

I screamed.

Annie swerved hard. I felt myself falling out through the open door. Peter grabbed my hands and held on with all his strength.

The car shot around the man and sped down the main street.

I saw the man shaking his big fist at us.

As the car roared away, I pulled myself onto the seat and slammed the back door. Peter and I sat there, shivering, silent. We were too frightened and too exhausted to speak.

"Annie, thank you for helping us," I said finally. I looked out the window. Whoa. Wait. Annie was driving us back up the hill.

"Where are we going?" I asked.

"Why are you taking us up the hill?" Peter demanded.

"I told you," Annie said. "I live on the hill, too."

Peter and I exchanged glances. He had a strong grip on the door handle. His face was tight with worry.

"Are you taking us to your house?" I asked.

She didn't answer.

The car followed the curving road, bumping over the ruts and holes. A short while later, Uncle Jonathan's house rose up in front of us.

"Hey! What's the big idea?" I shouted angrily.

Too late.

Annie stopped the car at the front door. Jonathan and Sonja stood waiting on the walk. Jonathan had a pleased smile under his black mustache.

He opened the back door. "Well, well," he said softly, "look who has returned."

Peter and I had no choice. We slid out of the car and stood facing Jonathan.

My heart was racing. I couldn't speak. I knew we'd been tricked. But — now what?

Annie stepped out from behind the wheel. Jonathan patted her on the shoulder. "Good work, Annie," he said. "I told you we needed someone in the village. Someone they trusted. Just in case they tried to escape."

"No problem, boss," Annie said, grinning.

"I . . . I don't understand," I stammered. "I don't —"

"You will soon," Jonathan replied.

He grabbed Peter by the shoulders. Sonja and Annie took me as their prisoner. They forced us into the house.

"Where are you taking us?" Peter cried.

"You'll recognize it," Jonathan said. "I saw you this morning. I know you've already visited my mummy museum."

They pushed us up the stairs, then guided us

to Jonathan's private quarters. Jonathan opened the door, and we stepped into the brightly lit mummy room.

The room rang out with loud moans and groans from the three rows of mummy cases. It sounded like a choir of sad, tortured voices.

I wanted to cover my ears. Were they suffering? Were they in pain?

How could two-thousand-year-old mummies be wailing and moaning in their cases?

I could feel all of my muscles tighten in fright. Beside me, Peter's face had gone green. I could see that he was terrified, too.

"Come along," Jonathan said brightly. He led us through the aisle of mummy cases to his white room at the back. "Come along. We have work to do."

Those words sent a cold shiver down my spine.

"Work?" I cried in a high, shrill voice. "Why are you doing this, Jonathan? What do you WANT?"

"I want your hair," Jonathan replied.

16

He turned and stared at me, and his eyes flashed with excitement. "I need your hair," he said. "The first time I saw it — in a photograph — I knew it would be right. But I tested it this morning. I cut off a lock and tested it. And it's PERFECT!"

My missing lock of hair. *Jonathan* cut it off?

"P-perfect?" I stammered.

The white room was spinning in front of me. I grabbed the edge of the metal table to keep from falling.

I felt dizzy. And confused. And terrified.

Jonathan was insane! Out of his mind. What did he want with my hair?

I reached up and pulled it behind my head, as if trying to protect it.

"What do you *mean*?" I cried. "Why do you want my hair?"

"I suppose I should explain," Jonathan said. He motioned to the table. "Sit down, Abby. I'll explain it all to you and your brother."

"Just let us go home!" Peter cried. "You can't keep us here."

Annie closed the door to the white room. She put her back against it, as if guarding it. Sonja stood stiffly beside her, hands at her waist.

Jonathan shook his head, a sad expression on his face. "You're wrong, Peter. I'm afraid I have to keep you two here — forever."

Peter swallowed. "That's one of your jokes — right?"

Jonathan turned to me. "You killed my cat, Abby," he said. "You saw her crumble to dust."

"Listen, I'm really sorry —" I started.

He raised a hand to silence me. "Cleopatra was an ancient cat," he said. "She was my cat for two thousand years. And you saw her crumble. You and Peter saw too much, Abby. That's why I couldn't let you leave — even if I *didn't* need your hair."

I just stared at him. Did any of this make sense?

Was he TOTALLY insane?

"I'm not crazy," Jonathan said.

Could he read my mind?

He pulled out his pipe and tapped it against the table. His eyes locked onto mine. "Sonja, Annie, and I don't come from your time," he said. "We are ancient Egyptians. We have found the secret of immortal life. We know how to stay alive forever."

"That's awesome," Peter said sarcastically. "Can we go home now?"

He started for the door, but Annie still stood in the way.

"You saw me in here with the mummy, didn't you, Abby?" Jonathan stepped up close to me. So close I could see the tiny beads of sweat on his forehead.

"And so you know how we stay alive," he continued. "We stay alive by eating the insides of mummies."

I pictured it again. Jonathan pushing that blobby, wet purple organ into his mouth. Once more, I felt my stomach lurch.

Jonathan opened a door at the back wall. He motioned for Peter and me to follow him.

He led us into a long, narrow white room with tall shelves on both sides. It seemed to be a storage room. As my eyes adjusted to the light, I saw mummies on the shelves.

The mummies lay on their backs. Two rows of them. Jonathan led us down the rows.

I pressed my hand to my mouth. I couldn't believe what I was seeing.

Their wrappings had all been opened.

Their insides were half eaten!

"Impossible!" I cried. The word burst from my throat. "You can't eat their insides. In two thousand years, their organs would all dry up. They'd be nothing but powder!"

A strange smile spread over Jonathan's face. "Two thousand years ago, I found the secret to keeping these mummies alive!" he cried. "I kept them alive all these years. Kept them alive so their organs would stay *fresh*!"

Down the rows, the mummies groaned and uttered sharp cries of pain. They didn't move. But the horrifying sounds rose from beneath their covered mouths.

"We won't tell anyone about this," Peter said in a tiny, frightened voice. "I promise. Not a word. Please — let us go."

"Yes, we'll just go home. We won't say anything," I said. I raised my hand. "I swear."

"You don't understand," Jonathan said softly. "The mummy organs keep us alive. But we need one special ingredient to keep the organs fresh enough to eat. Can you guess what that is?"

My hands flew up to my hair. "Oh, nooo," I moaned.

"Yes. You guessed it. I need a special protein from the hair of certain people. Our supply is running low. It's so lucky you two came along."

He pulled me out of the storage room and led me to the metal table. "Not just any hair. It has to be straight, jet-black hair with the special protein. You and your brother *both* have the protein I need."

"No, please —" I said.

Jonathan was surprisingly strong. He grabbed me under the arms and lifted me onto the table.

"You're going to grow beautiful hair for me," he said softly. "Beautiful hair to keep Annie, Sonja, and me alive. I'm so sorry, Abby. But I'm going to keep you and Peter here a long time — until your hair turns gray."

He pushed me down onto my back. He held me by the shoulders.

Across the room, I saw Sonja raise a big pair of silvery shears. As big as gardening shears! A grim smile spread across her wide face as she came toward me, holding the shears high.

And in the back room, I heard the mummies start to chant:

"HAIR! HAIR! HAIR! HAIR!"

Ancient voices croaking the word from somewhere deep in their throats. An animal sound, like bullfrogs at night.

"HAIR! HAIR! HAIR! HAIR!"

Sonja clicked the shears above me. Once. Twice.

Then she lowered them to my head.

17

"NOOOOOOOO!"

I let out a long scream. I jerked my shoulders up. Twisted hard. Tried to squirm out of Jonathan's grasp.

But Annie hurried over to the table to help hold me down.

"Let me go! You can't do this!" I shrieked.

Sonja clicked the heavy shears above my head. "You'd better be holding still, girl," she said. "Faith, you don't want to be losing an ear."

"You won't miss your hair for long," Annie said. "You'll have many months to grow a new batch for us."

"No — stop!" I pleaded.

Above my head, the shears slid open. Sonja lowered them slowly to my hair.

And then I saw Peter move.

He lowered his shoulder — and barreled into Jonathan. He caught Jonathan by surprise. Knocked the wind out of him.

Jonathan uttered a choked gasp. His hands fell away from me as he staggered back. He bent over, hands on his knees, struggling to breathe.

I rolled off the table before he could catch his breath.

Annie made a wild grab for me. Missed.

I dropped to the floor and took off toward the door.

"HAIR! HAIR! HAIR! HAIR!"

The mummies in the back room continued their ugly chant.

Jonathan stood up again, his face bright red, his eyes wild. He waved both arms frantically, signaling Annie and Sonja to chase after me.

Then he dove for Peter. Peter ducked away and raced to the door.

"HAIR! HAIR! HAIR! HAIR!" The weird, low voices rang in my ears.

We were almost out of the white room when the door swung open.

"Oh!" I cried out as a man stepped in and blocked our path.

"You!" Peter shouted.

The big, evil-looking man with the scar across his forehead. He wore a dark trench coat with the collar turned up to his face. His boots were splattered with mud.

He was breathing hard, sweating. His chest heaved up and down. His eyes darted furiously around the room.

Jonathan raised his fists as if preparing for a fight. Annie and Sonja dropped back, shock on their faces.

"How did you get in here?" Jonathan boomed.

The man didn't answer.

"Out! Get *out*!" Jonathan screamed.

"No. I'm taking the kids," the man said.

"You're not taking them," Jonathan said, stepping forward. "No way."

The big man stiffened his back, preparing for a fight.

Peter and I were stuck between them.

"Why are you after us?" I cried. "Who ARE you?"

The man narrowed his eyes at me. "I'm your Uncle Jonathan," he said.

18

"HAIR! HAIR! HAIR! HAIR!"

"I'm your Uncle Jonathan," the man repeated. He had to shout over the cry of the mummies. "This man is a *fraud*!" He took a menacing step toward Jonathan.

The man *we* knew as Jonathan backed up to the metal table. "You'll never take these kids from me," he said. "I need them."

I spun back and forth between them, trying to clear my head. Was the bald man telling the truth? Was he really our uncle?

"You might as well know the truth," the first Jonathan said, "since none of you are ever leaving this house."

He ran his hand back through his long hair. His eyes moved from the man at the door, back to Peter and me.

"My name is Tuttan-Rha," he said. "I told you before, my two friends and I come from the Egypt of two thousand years ago."

"You — you're really not our uncle? Then . . . how do you know us?" I asked. My voice came out in a trembling whisper. "How did you know to meet us at the train station?"

A strange smile spread over Tuttan-Rha's face. The smile pulled his skin tight over his cheekbones. It was like looking at his skull.

"I saw your uncle in the village a few weeks ago," he said. "He was showing off pictures of you. Pictures that your Granny Vee had sent him. I saw your long black hair in the pictures. I almost started to drool. I knew that I *needed* your hair. Needed it to *live!*"

Sonja nodded. She still held the shears in her hand. "Yes, we needed you. Such beautiful hair. So perfect."

"Your uncle's house is in the village," Tuttan-Rha said. "On the day you two arrived, I sent Sonja there to delay him. It was easy. While she kept Jonathan busy, I picked you up in the carriage and brought you here to my house."

"I got to the train station, and you weren't there," Jonathan said. "I was frantic. I was only twenty minutes late. Someone in the village told me you were taken to the weird house up on the hill."

He shook his head sadly. "The village has no police. No one to help me. I've been trying to get to you ever since."

"HAIR! HAIR! HAIR! HAIR!"

76

"Why won't they *stop*!" I cried.

"Let's get out of here," Uncle Jonathan said. He put a hand on our backs and started to push Peter and me out the door.

"Why waste your time? You'll never get out of this house," Tuttan-Rha called after us. "You remember the bats — don't you, Jonathan?"

Jonathan stopped in the doorway.

"I watched your first battle with them. It wasn't pretty. Do you really want to fight them again?" Tuttan-Rha asked. "I have them trained. When I give the signal, they will tear you to pieces."

Uncle Jonathan shuddered. I could see the fear on his face. He was thinking hard. Trying to come up with an escape plan.

Suddenly, I had an idea.

A crazy idea. But one that might just work.

"RUN!" I screamed.

19

I took off, and Jonathan and Peter followed. The mummies in the front room were chanting, too. We ran through the long aisle of mummy cases, reached the door, and burst through it.

"Peter —" I said breathlessly as we ran down the long hall. "Your water blaster. Get it."

"Huh?" He squinted at me. "Are you joking?"

"It melted Cleopatra," I said. "The water. It turned her to dust. Maybe it will do the same thing to Tuttan-Rha and the two women."

We ran into Peter's room.

"Maybe we should just make a run for it," Jonathan said. "Maybe the bats won't follow us. Maybe —"

"Tuttan-Rha said they would destroy us," I said. "We can't take that chance." I turned to Peter. He was frantically tossing clothes everywhere. "Where's your blaster?"

"I don't know!" he cried. "I can't find it. I thought I left it here on the floor."

I turned to the door. Tuttan-Rha would be here any second.

Peter crawled under the bed. "It isn't here!" he cried. "I can't find it."

"Never mind," I said, running from the room. "I'll get mine."

I darted into my room. Jonathan and Peter followed. The water blaster sat on my bedtable.

"Yess!" I cried. I grabbed it in both hands. I lifted it off the table.

Too light.

I shook it. "Empty," I muttered. I'd used up the whole tank on Cleopatra.

I heard heavy, thudding footsteps in the hall. Tuttan-Rha was just outside the door.

I dove into my bathroom. Spun the cold-water knob on the sink. My hand shook as I struggled to fill the water gun. Water sprayed everywhere.

I filled the gun almost full. Ran back into the bedroom. Handed it to Uncle Jonathan.

"Give them all a good blast," I said. "Maybe —"

I couldn't finish my sentence. Tuttan-Rha burst into the room, followed by Annie and Sonja. He came rushing at us. The two women blocked the doorway.

"Don't get your hopes up, kids," Tuttan-Rha said. "You're never leaving this house. You will stay and grow your wonderful hair for me and my friends."

"Don't get YOUR hopes up!" Jonathan declared. He raised the water blaster. Aimed it at Tuttan-Rha's chest.

I held my breath. Waiting to see what the spray of water would do to the ancient Egyptian.

But there *was* no spray of water.

Tuttan-Rha dove forward — and slapped the water blaster out of Jonathan's hands.

The plastic gun hit the wall and bounced onto the rug. I made a grab for it, but Crazy Annie got to it first.

Tuttan-Rha tackled Jonathan around the waist and dropped him to the floor. They began to wrestle, grunting and rolling around on the carpet.

The two women kept their eyes on the fight. But they didn't move from the door.

We were trapped.

I stood there helplessly. What could I do to help Jonathan?

The two men rolled around and around. They punched each other and drove their elbows into each other's chests.

Jonathan fought desperately. He was twice as big as Tuttan-Rha. But the ancient Egyptian had amazing strength.

He pinned Jonathan's shoulders to the floor. Then he took his arm and pressed it over Jonathan's throat.

Jonathan struggled to squirm out from under

the Egyptian's hold. But he wasn't strong enough.

Tuttan-Rha pressed his arm down harder. I could see that Jonathan couldn't breathe. He made horrible choking sounds, and his face turned bright purple.

I couldn't bear to watch. *How could I help?*

I knew I had to act fast.

I ran back to the bathroom.

A weak gurgle escaped Jonathan's throat. Then he was silent.

Tuttan-Rha raised his arm from Jonathan's throat and sat up. He had a broad smile on his face.

"You lose, Jonathan," he said. "Say good-bye to your niece and nephew."

20

Tuttan-Rha flashed Sonja and Annie a victory smile. His face was red, and his mustache was drenched with sweat.

Jonathan lay still on his back, eyes closed tightly. His arms lay limply on the floor at his sides.

Was he breathing? I couldn't tell.

Peter stood with his hands shoved deep in his jeans pockets. He pressed his back against the wall. His eyes were wide with fright.

I strode quickly from the bathroom, my eyes on Tuttan-Rha.

He turned to me. "Where were you, Abby? Did you think you could hide in the bathroom? Or were you too afraid to watch me defeat your uncle?"

I didn't reply.

Instead, I emptied my mouth. I'd filled it up in the bathroom sink. And now I did one of my champion, gold-medal water spits.

I spewed a hard stream of water from my mouth — and sprayed the ancient Egyptian in the face.

The water splashed onto his cheeks, his nose, his mustache. Then it ran down his chin onto his neck.

His mouth dropped open and he moaned.

His eyes bulged.

He let out a cry. But it was drowned out by a loud sizzling. It sounded like hamburgers frying on a grill.

Smoke poured off Tuttan-Rha's face as his skin started to burn. His hair crumbled to ashes. The whole front of his face peeled off, revealing gray bone underneath.

His ears fell off and dropped silently to the floor.

"*Unh . . . unh . . .*" He uttered two groans, the last sounds he'd ever make.

His skull crumbled to powder. And then, the rest of his body started falling apart, crumbling, disappearing into his clothes.

In seconds, I stared at a crumpled suit of clothes, covered in black and gray ashes.

Two eyeballs rolled off the jacket collar and came to rest on the carpet. They gazed up at me blankly. Then they, too, crumbled to powder.

"Abby — you were awesome!" Peter cried. "You did it!"

But I knew it was too soon to celebrate. I spun around to see what Sonja and Annie would do.

Would we have to fight them next?

No.

To my shock, their clothes lay in a heap on the bedroom floor. The two women had also crumbled to ashes. The ashes formed small pyramids on top of their clothes.

"All three of them must have been connected somehow," I said. "They shared a life force or something."

"Or something," a voice repeated. From the floor.

Tuttan-Rha? Had he come back to life?

I gasped and turned to the sound. And saw Uncle Jonathan struggling to sit up.

He shook his bald head, blinking his eyes. "I think I'm alive," he said groggily.

And then he saw the crumpled clothes, the piles of ashes. He squinted at me. "Abby?"

"They're gone," I said. "Please — let's get out of this creepy place."

Peter and I helped pull Jonathan to his feet. We stepped around the two ash pyramids and hurried into the hall.

"Which way?" Jonathan asked, gazing in one direction, then the other. "We'll have to walk down the hill. I parked my car at the bottom, and —"

"Wait!" I cried. "One more thing. We're forgetting the mummies."

I turned and started to jog toward Tuttan-Rha's private quarters. Peter and Jonathan followed.

"He kept the mummies alive all these years," I said. "They've been moaning and groaning in pain. What do we do with them now?"

I pulled open the door and burst into the huge mummy chamber. Pale sunlight from the tall windows poured over the rows of mummy cases.

I stopped. And listened for their sighs and groans.

No.

Silence. The room stood silent and still.

I turned to Peter and Jonathan. "Their life force must have been connected to Tuttan-Rha's, too," I said. "After two thousand years, these ancient mummies are finally at rest."

I couldn't resist. I walked up to the nearest mummy case. I leaned over the side and peered down at the mummy. Its arms were crossed. Its coverings were ragged and stained.

Leaning farther, I stared into its hidden face.

And its hands shot up. And *grabbed* my arms — and *tugged* me down on top of it!

21

I was too shocked and terrified to scream.

I felt its dry, bony arms wrap around my waist. I could smell the mold and mildew from thousands of years ago. So strong and sour, I choked.

I struggled to twist out of its grip.

Holding on to me tightly, it pulled itself up. It raised its head . . . and uttered a hoarse whisper in my ear:

"Thank you . . . Thank you."

Then I felt the strength fade from its body. It sank back into the case with a final sigh. Its arms fell limply to its sides.

My whole body shook and itched from its dry, scratchy touch. Choking on the foul odor, I gripped the sides of the case with both hands — and pushed myself out.

Peter and Jonathan grabbed my shoulders and stood me on my feet.

"Are you okay?" Jonathan asked.

I nodded. "He said thank you," I told him. "He only wanted to thank me for letting him die."

"*Now* can we go home?" Peter asked. "I want to go somewhere BORING!"

The next day at the Cranford train station, Jonathan apologized a thousand times. "I'm so sorry I wasn't there to meet you when you arrived," he said. "I'm so sorry you had to have such a *horrifying* time."

"I can't even tell my friends about it," Peter said. "Who would *believe* it?"

"Well, we had an adventure we'll never forget!" I said.

"Awesome, Abby," Peter said, rolling his eyes. "Always look on the bright side."

Jonathan helped us hoist our bags into the train car. "At least you're both safe and sound," he said.

He hugged us both. "Please give my warmest regards to Granny Vee," he said. "I hope she's okay."

"Me, too," I murmured.

The train started to move. Jonathan ran down the aisle and jumped off. He waved to us from the platform as we rolled past.

Peter and I settled back into our seats. It was going to be a long train trip back to Boston. But we'd never been happier to go home.

We lugged our bags into the front hall and ran into the living room.

"Granny Vee! Granny Vee?"

"Upstairs," she called. Her voice sounded light. Weak.

We found her tucked in bed. "You're back," she whispered.

She pulled herself to a sitting position.

I tried not to show how upset I was. But Granny Vee looked so weak and frail and tired. All the life had faded from her eyes. Her arms were as thin as toothpicks. And her face was as pale as flour.

She squeezed my hand. Peter and I hugged her and kissed her.

Our greeting seemed to tire her. She slumped back onto the pillow.

"I see you staring at me," she said with a thin smile. "Well, I guess I can't hide the truth from you two. I'm not doing well. Not doing well at all."

"We'll help you," Peter said. "We'll help you get better."

I started to pull her up. "Don't worry, Granny Vee," I said. "I brought something home with me to make you feel better."

Peter took one hand and I took the other. We guided her out of the bedroom.

"Where are you taking me?" Granny Vee asked.

"You'll see," I said. "Come sit down."

"You're being very mysterious," Granny Vee said.

"Don't ask questions," I said.

We sat her down at the kitchen table. I unpacked the parcel I'd brought from the village.

I brought it to the table and started to unwrap the paper around it.

"What is it?" Granny Vee asked. She sniffed the air. "Oh. What a strong smell."

I spread out the paper and set it down in front of her.

She gazed at it, blinking hard. "What is that, Abby? Some kind of liver?" She made a face. "I don't like the smell of it."

"Don't pay attention to the smell," I said. I picked it up and put it in her hand. "Just eat a nice chunk. It will do you a world of good!"

"But what *is* it?" Granny Vee demanded.

"I'll tell you after you eat a piece," I said. "Go ahead." I pushed it into her mouth. "I promise, Granny Vee. You're gonna be around for a *long, long* time!"

ENTER HORRORLAND

THE STORY SO FAR...

Several kids received mysterious invitations to be Very Special Guests at HorrorLand theme park. They looked forward to a week of scary fun — but the scares quickly became TOO REAL.

Two girls — Britney Crosby and Molly Molloy — disappeared. Billy Deep was horrified when his sister, Sheena, became invisible. Then Sheena disappeared, too, for a short while.

A park guide — a Horror named Byron — warned the kids they were all in danger. Byron tried to help them. But then he was dragged away by other Horrors.

Why are they all in danger? Where are the two missing girls? The kids are desperate to find Byron to get some answers.

Meanwhile, Abby Martin arrives a few days after the others. Abby is eager to put her mummy nightmares behind her and have some fun. She has no idea of the terrifying dangers that await her.

Abby continues the story. . . .

1

When Granny Vee showed me the invitation, I was shocked. "Peter and I? Invited to HorrorLand? For free?" I cried. "Are you sure the invitation is for *us*?"

"It has your name right on it, Abby," Granny Vee said. "You must have won a contest or something."

It was four months after our adventure in Cranford with the mummies. Granny Vee was looking young and strong. But Peter and I still had problems.

Peter crossed his arms in front of him. "I'm not going," he said. "No way."

"Why not?" I demanded. "It's supposed to be the scariest, most awesome theme park on earth."

"I just don't want to," Peter said, whining. "I want to hang out with my friends."

I knew what the problem was. Peter was afraid. Ever since we returned from Tuttan-Rha's terrifying house, Peter was frightened by a lot of things. He didn't even want to have water-gun fights.

Who could blame him?

I still dreamed about the chanting mummies at night. In my dreams, I heard their frightening moans and cries. Some nights, I woke up with the ugly ancient voices chanting *"HAIR! HAIR! HAIR!"* in my ears.

I decided that a week in HorrorLand might be a chance to escape my nightmares.

I tried hard to persuade Peter to come with me. But he was totally stubborn. So I ended up going to HorrorLand without him.

Did I escape my nightmares?

Three guesses. The first two don't count.

My first night in HorrorLand in the Stagger Inn, I had a terrifying dream. I saw myself back in my room at Tuttan-Rha's house.

I was lying in the canopy bed with the purple curtains. The window was open, and I could hear flapping bat wings outside.

I sat up. And saw a mummy case at the foot of the bed.

The case was decorated with carvings of strange birds and cats. A pharaoh's death mask was sculpted on the lid.

As I stared, the lid began to move. It made a loud grinding sound as it slid open.

I covered my ears. I didn't want to hear it.

I knew I was dreaming. I tried to wake up. Tried to pull myself out of the dream, out of that horrid room.

But the bed held me down. Like a soft trap.

I stared as the lid opened all the way. Bandaged arms reached up from inside the case. The wrappings were stained and torn.

The mummy stretched, clenching and unclenching its bony fingers. The fingers crackled with each move.

The dry sound made my stomach lurch.

I shut my eyes. *Abby, wake up*, I told myself in the dream. *Wake up. Please!*

I opened my eyes, hoping to be back in my own room at Granny Vee's house. But no. Cracking and groaning, the mummy lifted itself from its case.

I forced myself out of the bed. My nightshirt was twisted around me. I tried to run to the door. I wanted to escape.

But to my horror, I was moving in slow motion.

I felt so heavy, as if I weighed five hundred pounds. I moved slowly. I seemed to be running in place.

The mummy staggered toward me. Its hands were stretched out as if preparing to wrap me in its arms.

The dream was so vivid, so real, I could *smell* the mummy. It had a sickeningly sweet odor, like rotting apples.

It groaned with each heavy, thudding step. It backed me into a corner.

I couldn't escape. Couldn't *wake up*!

It reached out. Raised one bony, ragged arm. Reached up, and I felt its dry, pawlike hand scrape my throat.

Ohhh, sick.

It rubbed its fingers over my cheek. I could feel my skin prickle.

It's only a dream, I told myself. So why did the touch of the mummy's hand on my face feel so *real*?

I woke up — screaming.

I was flat on my back. My whole body trembled. My mouth was dry. I struggled to slow my breathing down to normal.

Why could I still feel the mummy's dry touch?

Blinking in the dark hotel room, it took me so long to realize that the window curtain was blowing over my face.

I sat up. Pushed the curtain away.

I started to feel a little better. *Just a window curtain. No need to panic, Abby. You had a bad dream, and a curtain touched your face.*

No biggie — right?

I lowered my feet to the floor. Still feeling shaky, I started to stand up.

I lowered my eyes — and gasped.

Were those footprints on the carpet? Yes. Muddy footprints from the door to my bed.

And what was that on the floor? I bent and picked it up. I raised it close to see it in the dim light.

A strip of stained, yellowed gauze.

I shuddered.

Someone had been in my room. Someone was playing a mean joke.

Did someone know about my mummy nightmares?

I gazed at the muddy footprints.

Who would try to scare me like this? Was this supposed to be part of the HorrorLand fun?

I stood up and straightened my nightshirt. I took a deep breath.

And heard thudding footsteps. Out in the hall.

And then a pounding knock on my door.

The mummy had returned!

Cut it out, Abby. I scolded myself. *Don't get crazy.*

I stepped to the door. "Who is it?" I called.

"I . . . I'm in the next room." A boy's voice. "Are you okay? I heard you scream."

I can't believe he heard that.

I pulled open the door. And stared at a boy about my age. He was big and tall, maybe a foot taller than me. He had short black hair, sort of a bulldog face, big brown eyes.

He was barefoot. He had a long T-shirt pulled down over pajama bottoms.

"I . . . woke up when I heard you scream," he said. "I thought . . ."

"I'm okay," I told him. "Guess I was having a nightmare."

He said his name was Michael Munroe. And he was a Very Special Guest, too.

We started talking, standing in the doorway. He said he was happy to get away from home and come to HorrorLand. He said he had a weird year at school.

"I had a weird year, too," I said. I had the sudden urge to tell him about the mummies and everything. But I stopped myself.

I knew he wouldn't believe it. He'd just think I was crazy.

He came in, and we sat down on the little couch by my window. "Do kids call you Mike or Michael?" I asked.

"Well . . . neither. The kids back at home call me Monster."

I laughed. "They call you Monster because . . . ?"

"I guess because I'm such a big dude. And sometimes I lose it. You know. Get angry."

He blushed. "I used to like that nickname," he said. "But . . . I had a thing with some *real* monsters. Now I hate that name."

Real monsters? Was he joking?

Maybe we both had the same kind of frightening year, I thought.

I liked him. He was kind of cute. And easy to talk to.

"Are you into sports?" I asked. "Wrestling or football?"

Michael shrugged. "Not really. I'm on the wrestling team. But actually, I'm kind of a techie. I'm into computers and stuff."

He scratched his short spiky hair. "What's up with this hotel?" he asked. "My cell phone won't work. And there's no Internet connection. I feel like a prisoner!"

"I just got here yesterday," I said. "I didn't try to call anyone."

I thought of Granny Vee. She'd be worried if I didn't call her today.

"It's like they don't want us to talk to anyone in the outside world," Michael said. "Or am I just being paranoid?"

"You're being paranoid," I said.

We both laughed. We talked for another hour. I felt like I'd made a new friend.

Later, after breakfast, we met up to explore the park. It was only ten o'clock, but people were starting to pour in.

"What a beautiful day!" I exclaimed. I was feeling good. Last night's nightmare had faded into the past.

The sun was still climbing through a clear blue sky. The air was warm and fresh. Kids were laughing and running ahead of their parents, eager to see everything.

A long line of people was waiting at a breakfast-food cart in the middle of Zombie Plaza. The cart was called AWFUL WAFFLE. And the Horror working there was serving waffles shaped like fat cockroaches.

"Want that with Skin Rash Syrup?" he asked a kid. "We squeeze it from poison ivy plants." He poured the syrup. I could see little black things swimming in it.

Yum!

"Did you meet any other Very Special Guests?" Michael asked.

I shook my head. "Not yet."

"I wonder if there are any more of us here," he said. He pointed. "Hey — look. Some cool rides. Let's do it!"

I started to follow him. He was so tall and took such long strides, it was hard to keep up.

I stopped when I saw a game booth at the edge of the plaza. I uttered a sharp cry. I felt the back of my neck tighten as I stared at it.

THE MUMMY'S TUMMY.

That's what the game was called. THE MUMMY'S TUMMY. In big, black Egyptian-style letters.

"Huh?" My mouth dropped open. I just stood there gaping at it.

And watched kids step up to a giant mummy. The mummy was at least eight feet tall, standing with its legs wide apart, arms crossed over its chest. Ragged gauze fluttered in the soft morning breeze.

When they got to the front of the line, kids reached a hand into the mummy's belly — and pulled out prizes.

My whole body shuddered.

How can this BE?

I guess Michael saw that I was freaked. "Abby, what's up?" he asked. "What's wrong?"

I shook my head as if trying to shake away what I was seeing. "N-nothing," I stammered. "I . . . can't explain."

First, the mummy footprints and gauze on my floor last night . . .

. . . Now this mummy game!

It CAN'T all be a coincidence.

Michael grabbed my hand and pulled me up to the giant mummy. He was so strong, I couldn't pull back.

"What's scary about *this* thing?" Michael asked. "Abby, you're shaking!"

"Uh . . . just a chill, I guess," I said. I tried not to stare at the big hole in the mummy's belly.

"Look. Nothing scary about it," Michael said.

He made a fist, then shoved his hand deep into the opening in the mummy's stomach.

He turned to me. "See?" he said. "No problem."

But then his expression changed. "Hey!" he shouted.

His eyes bulged. His mouth dropped open. "My hand!" he cried.

Struggling to pull out his hand, Michael shut his eyes and let out a shriek of pain and horror.

I let out a cry and staggered back from the mummy.

A grin spread over Michael's face. He slid his hand out.

"Just goofing," he said.

He let out a big laugh. I forced a smile, but I didn't exactly feel like laughing.

Why is this thing here?

It *couldn't* have been set up in the middle of the park just to scare *me* — could it?

We walked past the mummy. "Wow. It's all like ancient Egypt back here," Michael said, gazing around.

I saw a yellow pyramid rising over a patch of sand. A giant sphinx statue guarded an ancient-looking temple.

I grabbed Michael's arm and tried to tug him in the other direction. "Let's get out of here," I said. "I want to see the Werewolf Petting Zoo. And —"

"No, wait." He slid out of my grasp. He pointed. "Check it out! An Egyptian roller coaster — and the cars are mummy cases! It looks totally awesome!"

He jogged over to it. I just wanted to run. I'd seen enough mummy cases to last my whole life.

But what could I do? I followed him.

The coaster was called The A-Nile-Ator.

Kids were running to get on the ride. They lay on their backs in the mummy cases. One kid per case.

Then the cases rolled up the tracks, slowly at first ... up ... up ... a steep climb. At the top, the cars spun around a tall yellow pyramid and whipped down, then up, twisting and turning, faster and faster.

Wild screams rang out from the cases as they whipped and spun around the giant pyramid. I couldn't see the riders, but it sounded like they were having good, scary fun.

"Let's do it!" Michael said, jumping up and down like a little kid.

"No. Really —" I started to protest.

I held my ears to shut out the screams of the kids above us. And when I did, I heard the moans and cries of pain of Tuttan-Rha's *real* mummies in their cases.

I put my hands down. Michael pulled me toward the ride. Before I knew it he was pushing me into a mummy case.

I took a deep breath and slid in. I settled onto my back and grabbed the safety handles at the sides.

The tall yellow pyramid cast a deep shadow over me. I heard kids screaming and laughing.

"I can do this," I told myself out loud. "I can do this ride. I'm not going to be scared for the rest of my life."

With a hard rumble, my case started to move. The bottom vibrated as I began the slow trip up to the top.

My feet were tilted up. My head slanted down. I could feel the blood rushing to my face.

I gripped the sides tightly as the mummy case picked up speed. I pictured Michael in the case behind me. He was probably doing it no-hands!

And then I heard his shout: "Abby, how are you doing?"

I started to answer — but the case whipped around hard, taking my breath away.

I shot straight down — headfirst! The strong wind blew my hair in every direction. The force of the wind was so powerful, it was hard to breathe.

I was gasping when the case stopped its drop and began to rise again.

The case spun hard. My feet rose high now, my head dipped down low. I gripped the side handles.

We climbed. Higher . . . higher . . .

I felt the warm sun on my face. The blue sky looked close enough to touch.

Higher . . .

And then I let out a sharp cry as my case started to tilt.

Was this part of the ride?

The mummy case was rolling over.

It was turning upside down!

"Noooo!" I uttered a frightened cry.

It turned onto its side. It was going to roll over and dump me out!

The safety belt!

Did I forget to strap it on?

There *has* to be a safety belt.

I let go of one side and began frantically searching underneath me. My hand pawed the bottom of the case.

No safety belt?

Nothing to hold me in. *Nothing!*

With a loud squeak, the car flipped upside down.

I could see the ground *miles* below.

I hung there upside down for a second or two.

And then my hands slipped off the handles — and I started to fall.

4

I heard a loud *snap*.

And I felt something wrap around my chest and waist.

Safety bars! Steel safety bars snapped over me and held me tightly in the case.

I was too shocked to laugh or cry out. Too shocked to *breathe*!

I heard kids screaming all around me. They just had the scare of their lives, too!

Slowly, my mummy case tilted right side up. I let out a long sigh. I was gripping the safety bars so hard, my hands ached.

The case rolled slowly back to the ground. Two tall Horrors, dressed in green-and-purple costumes, appeared. All the park workers were called Horrors. They helped lift me out and stand me back on my feet. "How was it?" one Horror asked. "Are you going to ride it again?"

"I don't think so," I said.

He looked disappointed.

I took a few wobbly steps. My legs felt shaky. My heart was still pounding.

A few seconds later, Michael came running over, a big grin on his face. "Awesome — right?" he cried. "I really thought I was going to fall out. Ready to do it again?"

I squinted at him. "You're joking — right?"

He laughed. "Abby, how'd you get to be such a scaredy-cat?" He didn't wait for an answer. "I'll do *anything* — you know? Guess that's why my friends call me Monster."

"Well, Monster, I want to go back to Stagger Inn," I said. "Get myself together. Maybe have some lunch."

He nodded. "No problem. Actually, I want to try my laptop again. There's *gotta* be a way to get online."

We started walking toward the hotel. The park was jammed with people. The sun beat down. I realized I was sweating.

I looked for a cart selling cold drinks. We passed a purple-and-green cart with flat pieces of meat piled up on the front. On the side of the cart, a sign read: FROSTED PIG PIECES. CHOCOLATE, STRAWBERRY, VANILLA.

Gross.

No one was standing in line for those tasty items.

Two headless men walked by in gray business suits. They held their heads in front of them in

110

both hands. The heads were singing, *"Don't worry, be happy."*

Michael and I both laughed at that. We stopped as a tall Horror stepped in front of us. He stuck out his big, pawlike hands to stop us.

The Horror's short yellow horns curled above the wavy green hair on his head. He had blue eyes under thick brown eyebrows. His whole body seemed to be covered with purple fur.

Was it a costume? It had to be. The Horrors weren't real. But then, why couldn't I see any eye holes in his mask? And how come I couldn't see any wrinkles in the fur?

"Who are you?" he demanded in a tense whisper. His eyes darted all around, as if he was watching out for something or someone.

I gazed at the brass name tag pinned to his overall strap: BYRON.

He leaned over me, casting a shadow over us both. "Are you Abby Martin?" He turned to Michael. "Michael Munroe?"

"Yes," I answered. "Is something wrong?"

I thought of Granny Vee. Was she sick again? Was he delivering a message from her?

"There's plenty wrong," Byron replied.

He glanced all around again. This dude was definitely TENSE.

He shoved something into my hand. "Someone wants you to have this," he whispered.

"Excuse me?" I said. "What is it?"

But he had already spun away from us and was trotting through the crowd on the plaza.

"Well, that was totally disturbing," Michael said. He grabbed my hand. "What is it? What did he give you?"

I gazed at the folded-up paper in my hand. "Oh, wow," I said. "I think it's just an ad. I saw other Horrors passing out flyers. For the magic show at the Haunted Theater."

"Big whoop," Michael muttered. "That dude looked so frightened, I thought it was going to be something really scary."

"He's just a good actor," I said.

I unfolded the sheet of paper. I was wrong. It *wasn't* an ad for the Haunted Theater. It was a handwritten note in red marker, and it read:

ESCAPE HORRORLAND.

YOU ARE IN DANGER.

Michael laughed. "That Horror probably goes around the park passing these out all day."

I stared at the fat red letters. Red as blood.

"I don't think so," I said. "Michael, he wasn't passing this out at random. He . . . he knew our names."

Michael rolled his eyes. "It's another HorrorLand joke. Like that roller coaster ride back there. We thought we were going to fall out and drop to the ground — but we didn't. They want to scare us. That's the whole fun of HorrorLand."

I thought hard. "I'm not so sure."

And then I saw Byron across the plaza.

I grabbed Michael's sleeve and pointed. "There he is. Come on. Let's make him tell us what this note is about."

I gripped the note tightly in my right hand, and we started to run. We almost crashed into two women pushing baby strollers. Then we got trapped in the middle of a group of teenagers heading to the games arcade.

We were both breathing hard by the time we caught up to him.

The tall Horror had his back to us. He was straightening the straps on his overalls as he gave directions to a family.

"Byron!" I called.

He spun around — and Michael and I both gasped.

5

The Horror blinked at us in surprise. Beneath his horns, he had yellow spiky hair. He stared at us with one green eye and one brown eye.

He wasn't Byron.

I squinted at his name tag: CODY.

"Oh, wow. Sorry," I muttered.

"Thought you were someone else," Michael said.

"That happens to me a lot," Cody said. "But you can always recognize me by the dimples in my cheeks. No one has dimples like these. I made them myself with a power drill."

He laughed.

I stared hard, but I didn't even *see* any dimples. I guessed it was his little joke.

He lowered his weird-colored eyes to the sheet of paper. "What's that?" he asked.

He didn't wait for an answer. He grabbed it from my hand and quickly read it.

I saw his expression change. His smile faded as he read it again. He squinted at it, studying it for a long time.

Then he laughed. "You two didn't *believe* this dumb warning, did you?" he asked.

"Well . . ." I started.

"It's one of our joke messages," he said. "You know, *nothing* is real at HorrorLand." He gave us a wave of his paw. "Have fun, guys! Don't get *too* scared! Ha-ha!"

He started to walk away.

"Hey, can we have that paper back?" Michael called.

Cody turned and shrugged his big furry shoulders. "I think I'll keep it. You know. Pass it on to some other sucker!"

He laughed again. "We Horrors pass these things out all day long. Part of our job. Gotta keep it SCARY! You know."

He turned and hurried away.

Michael and I stared at each other. "Well, *that* was disturbing," I said.

"I told you," Michael said. "I told you it was just a joke."

I groaned. "Are you kidding me? Michael, that Horror was *totally* lying. Didn't you hear that phony laugh?"

Michael shrugged. "I believed him, Abby. Why would someone send us a threat like that? We

115

just got here. Why would someone want us out? We were invited!"

Of course, I didn't have answers to those questions.

Michael and I discussed the warning note all the way back to Stagger Inn.

As we walked, we passed groups of kids and dozens of families, all laughing and having fun. None of them seemed afraid. I didn't see any of them carrying handwritten messages in red ink.

"See you later," I told Michael. I took the dark, creaky elevator up to my room.

The elevator was ice-cold. Frightening organ music played as it climbed. And I shared the elevator with a skeleton, who was leaning against the back wall, holding a suitcase.

I stepped into my room and found my cell phone on the nightstand. I picked it up. I started to call Granny Vee.

Silence.

No bars. No network here.

"Weird," I muttered. I set it back down. Started to the closet. And spotted something on the desk.

A folded-up sheet of white paper.

My breath caught in my throat.

I hurried over to it and picked it up. My hands trembled as I struggled to unfold it.

Another threat!

No. Wait.

My eyes glanced over the page. There were bats with red eyes all around the margins.

Did someone know how much I hated bats?

No. It was an invitation. To lunch. I read it carefully:

Come meet all the Very Special Guests at the Vampire Café.
All blood types are welcome!
Get the 4-1-1 at a meeting afterwards —
unless you are feeling DRAINED!

There was a little square map at the bottom of the page. I saw that the Vampire Café was in the Vampire State Building.

Sounded like fun. And I was eager to meet the others. Mainly, I was curious. I wanted to ask them why they were picked as Very Special Guests.

I glanced at my watch. Almost lunchtime.

I hurried into the bathroom to get ready. My long hair had been blown in every direction by that roller coaster ride. It was a tangled mess. I grabbed my hairbrush.

"Huh?" No mirror in the bathroom?

That's totally weird, I thought.

I moved back into the bedroom and searched around. No dresser mirror. No wall mirror.

I pulled open the closets. No mirrors on the closet doors.

A hotel room without a single mirror?

Shaking my head, I walked to the window. I could see my reflection just a little bit in the glass. I brushed my hair as best as I could. Then I changed into a fresh T-shirt and shorts.

I grabbed the invitation and headed out the door.

I heard flapping bat wings as I stepped into the Vampire Café.

Abby, don't freak, I told myself. I took a deep breath. *The bats aren't real here. Nothing is real.*

I stepped up to the hostess. The room was so dark, I could barely see her. She raised a candle and smiled at me in the flickering light. She was very pale, with black lips and heavy black eyeliner around her eyes.

She wore a long black dress and a black cape

that brushed the floor as she stepped forward. "Welcome," she said softly. "We keep it very dark because the vampires burn up in bright light. And I *hate* when that happens."

"I like your eye makeup," I said.

She squinted at me. "I don't wear makeup."

The flapping bat wings grew louder. They sounded as if they were right overhead.

I knew it was just sound effects. But I still felt a chill.

The hostess led me to a long table at the back. A waitress was filling everyone's glass from a big pitcher. The drink was red and thick. Like *blood*? "We only serve it warm," she told me. "More nourishing that way, don't you think?"

Before I could answer, a boy jumped up and started introducing everyone around the table. It was hard to remember all the names.

I sat down next to a pretty girl with straight brown hair named Carly Beth. The boy who greeted me was tall and athletic looking. I think his name was Matt. Next to him — a brother and sister named Billy and Sheena.

I dropped into my chair. The waitress filled my glass. I tasted it. Tomato juice.

Against the far wall, I saw a tree. Fake, I guessed. And hanging from the branches of the tree were dozens of bats. I hoped they were fakes, too.

I waved to Michael. He sat at the other end of the long table, next to a boy whose name I think was Robby. Robby was busily drawing a cartoon on his placemat, and Michael was laughing.

"Have you all been here a long time?" I asked. "Has it been awesome?"

"Definitely not awesome," Matt replied. "We've had some . . . problems."

"I was telling Matt what Sabrina and I overheard," Carly Beth said. She leaned closer so everyone could hear her over the noise of the restaurant.

"We heard these two Horrors talking," Carly Beth said. "One of them was named Bubba. I don't remember the second one. They didn't know we were there."

"And what did they say?" Robby asked, putting down his marker.

"They were talking about us. The Very Special Guests," Carly Beth said. "They said it's going to get a lot scarier for us."

"They didn't mean it as a joke," the girl named Sabrina said. "They meant it for real."

I glanced around the table. The kids all looked weird in the flickering candlelight. But even in the darkness, I could see how troubled they were.

Matt shook his head. "Byron warned us we weren't safe," he said. "We have to keep searching for him. If we can find him, he'll tell us what's really going on here."

"Hey," I said. "Did you say Byron? I just saw a Horror named Byron."

The kids all acted shocked. A few of them gasped.

Everyone at the table turned to me. "Where did you see him?" Sheena asked.

"Was he okay?" her brother, Billy, asked.

They bombarded me with questions. "Do you know where he went? Did he give you a message for us? Did he tell you anything?"

I was totally confused. Why were they so excited about this Horror named Byron?

"He came up to Michael and me at Zombie Plaza," I said. "And he —"

"He gave Abby a message," Michael interrupted. "It said, ESCAPE HORRORLAND. YOU ARE IN DANGER."

"We didn't know if it was a joke or not," I said. "We tried to find Byron to explain, but he disappeared in the crowd."

That got everyone buzzing.

"Let's go," Matt said. He stood up. "If he's walking around the park, we have to find him. We have to learn the truth."

Carly Beth pulled Matt back down into his seat. "We can't just run out," she said. "There's a meeting after lunch, remember?"

"Maybe we can ask questions," Sabrina said. "Maybe we can get some answers at the meeting."

Everyone started talking at once.

Robby clinked his spoon against his glass until we grew quiet. "I didn't get to tell my story," he said. "I saw the two missing girls. In the arcade."

The kids all acted stunned again.

Michael and I stared at each other across the table. We were both totally confused. Missing girls? What were they *talking* about?

"They came into the arcade. Really," Robby said, tapping his marker excitedly on the tabletop. "I saw them both. I talked with them."

"What did they say?" Matt asked him.

"That none of us are safe in HorrorLand," Robby answered. "They wanted to take me to another park. They said we'd be safe there."

"That *proves* it!" Matt cried. "We have to get *out* of here!"

"Wait a minute! Wait a minute!" Sabrina cried. Everyone turned to her. "Robby hit his head. When Carly Beth and I found him in the arcade, he was totally unconscious."

"So?" Robby demanded.

"So maybe you dreamed about seeing Britney and Molly," Carly Beth said.

"Right," Sabrina agreed. "You were knocked out. How could you see the two girls?"

"Whoa. Wait." Robby stood up and reached into his jeans pockets. "I didn't dream it. I can prove it."

He pulled a golden coin from his pocket and held it up. "Check it out," he said. "They gave this to me. It says PANIC PARK on it. It's some kind of token from another park."

He passed the coin around. Everyone studied it with serious expressions.

Again, I glanced across the table at Michael. He and I didn't know what they were talking about. *Missing girls? Another theme park?*

I had a million questions I wanted to ask them.

The token came to me. I raised it close to my face to study it. It was shiny and new. I could see the letters PP engraved on one side.

And I could see my reflection in the coin. I saw my eye up close. Then I saw that one side of my hair was messed up.

Suddenly, I felt a strong pull.

As if the coin were pulling me toward it. Like a vacuum cleaner.

I blinked. *What is up with this?*

I gripped the coin tightly. I tried to pull back.

But I could feel myself sliding . . . moving toward the shiny surface . . .

It was drawing me to it . . . pulling me . . . pulling me *into* it.

I felt so strange, so helpless and light.

7

A hand grabbed the token away.

I felt dizzy, stunned. I turned to see that the waitress had taken it. She shoved it into her black apron pocket.

"Thanks for the tip, guys," she said. "Tips mean a lot to us."

Robby jumped to his feet and stuck out his hand. "Hey, give it back!" he cried. "That wasn't your tip. That token belongs to *me*!"

The waitress rolled her eyes. "Okay, okay," she grumbled. "Don't get your boxers in a twist." She handed back the token.

Robby raised it to his face to examine it in the candlelight. "Hey!" he shouted. "It's not the same coin. This one says HorrorLand on it."

He turned around to protest. But the waitress had disappeared into the kitchen.

"She made a switch!" Robby cried. "She didn't want us to have that token."

"Let's go get her!" Matt declared. He jumped up, too.

But before anyone could move from the table, two Horrors stepped up to block our way.

One of them was a skinny Horror with purple freckles on his green face. His name tag read: BUBBA. The other was the yellow-haired Horror, Cody.

"Hope you all enjoyed your *last meal* on earth!" Bubba boomed.

He was joking. The two Horrors led us to a big dimly lit auditorium for our meeting. The stage was lit by one spotlight. It beamed down on a podium in front of a black curtain.

We Very Special Guests filled the front row. The rest of the auditorium was empty. Eerie organ music played over the speakers. The two Horrors took up places at the doors. Were they guarding the exits?

Michael and I sat at one end of the row. Next to us, Robby was showing his token to Billy and Sheena.

"Do you get what they were talking about?" Michael asked. "Something about two girls named Britney and Molly? And they went missing?"

Before I could answer, a smiling Horror walked across the stage and stepped into the spotlight. He was very thin and frail looking. He had pale green skin, a bald head under his horns, and squinted down at us through square-framed glasses.

"My name is Ned," he said in a squeaky old man's voice. "We're so happy to have you all in our park. We invited you as Very Special Guests for a reason. We want you to go home and tell all your friends how much good, scary fun you had at HorrorLand. And tell them to come visit us, too."

"But someone is really trying to scare us!" Matt shouted from his seat.

Ned's smile grew even wider. "All in good fun," he said.

Matt didn't give up. "We have a lot of questions for you," he said.

Ned nodded. "I'll be happy to answer your questions," he squeaked. "But first, I have a special gift for each of you. A little memento of your stay with us."

Matt groaned. "This dude won't answer anything," he muttered.

"Here to give you your gifts," Ned said, "is the Horror who had the great idea to invite you all here to the park. And it was his idea to have this meeting today." He waved to the side of the stage. "Please come here and hand out the gifts."

A tall Horror with short yellow horns, green hair, and purple fur came striding out, carrying a package.

Byron!

I recognized him instantly — the Horror who gave me that warning message. The other kids were all muttering excitedly.

"We've been looking *everywhere* for him," I heard Sheena whisper. "And here he is!"

"Byron — where *were* you?" Matt shouted.

Ned stood beside Byron, a smile pasted on his face. Byron pretended he didn't hear Matt's question.

He held up the package. "I have special HorrorLand tokens for each of you," he said. "I think you will want to carry them with you everywhere."

"It will show the Horrors around the park that you are a Very Special Guest," Ned said. "No more standing in line. Just show your token and go right in."

"And food is *free* at all our restaurants," Byron added. "Just show your special token."

"Byron will call you up one by one to receive your gift," Ned announced.

Byron called me up first. I took the coin from him and went back to my seat. When I looked at it, I had a shock.

The token had a pyramid on it!

"Huh?" My mouth dropped open.

Why did I get an Egyptian one? Do they know about the mummies in my uncle's village?

Wait. Did all the kids get pyramid tokens?

No. Matt's token had a weird blob on it. Carly Beth's had an ugly Halloween mask. Robby's had a cartoon superhero.

Everyone seemed shocked and upset.

Did the other kids have something horrifying happen to them, too?

Is that what they see on their coins?

"We have a lot of questions!" Matt shouted up to the stage.

But Ned turned and walked off quickly. Byron started to follow him.

But then he turned back to us. And in a loud whisper, he said: "Inside the Bat Barn. Four o'clock sharp."

I followed the other kids out into the afternoon sunlight. The park was crowded with people having fun. Across from us, a Horror in a clown suit was making balloon animals for little kids. The balloon animals all looked like *rats*.

We gathered under the shade of a big tree, and we all started talking at once.

"Something really scary happened to me," I said. "With real mummies. And look at my token." I held it up so they could see the pyramid on it.

The others all chimed in. Their tokens matched what happened to them during the year.

"It's totally disturbing," Billy said. "How could our worst nightmares follow us here?"

Michael had been quiet. I saw him studying his token intently. Suddenly, he let out a cry. "Look at this!"

We all turned and watched him pull a tiny chip from his coin. "I've seen this before. It's a tracking device," Michael said. "I bet they want to spy on us and track our every move."

"We've got to lose these," Robby said. "Right now."

"But wait —" Carly Beth said. "You say you trust this Byron guy, right? He's on *our* side? So if these really are tracking chips, they are a *good* idea!"

"Yes, we should keep them if Byron wants us to have them," Sabrina said.

"No way!" Matt declared. "Don't you see? They *forced* Byron to give us these things. That's why he wants to meet us later."

"I know about this electronic spying stuff," Michael said. "No one is going to track me! I'll show you what to do with these coins."

He walked over to a redheaded kid who was slurping an ice-cream cone with his mom. He handed the coin to the kid. "It makes you a special visitor," he said. "You can use it to get free food and stuff."

"Cool! Thanks!" the kid exclaimed. He took the coin and showed it off to his mom.

So that's what we did. We all gave our coins away to passing kids. Everyone except Carly Beth and Sabrina, that is. They kept theirs.

It was almost four o'clock. We hurried across the park to the Bat Barn. A fat, purple Horror greeted us at the entrance. He handed us all wide-brimmed hats. "It might keep the bats out of your hair!" he said.

I realized I was trembling. I wished I didn't have to go into the Bat Barn.

We started into the long, dark building. Chittering bat cries rang out above our heads. I could see bats hanging upside down from the low rafters.

I looked away — and saw a piece of paper on the floor.

I picked it up and held it close to my eyes. It was hard to read in the little bit of light that crept into the barn.

Michael stepped up beside me, and I showed it to him. "It looks like a page from an amusement park guide," I said.

We both stared at it. It showed kids in an old-fashioned Hall of Mirrors.

The headline read:

WELCOME TO THE MIRROR MANSION. *Reflect on Where It Can Take You!*

We passed it around. "Byron must have left this for us," Billy said. "It *has* to be some kind of clue — like the other pages we found."

His sister, Sheena, started to say something. But instead, a scream burst from her mouth.

And seconds later, we ALL began to scream as the bat attack began.

Bats swooped down on us — dozens of them. Screeching and whistling. Flapping furiously.

I tugged the hat down low on my head and gripped the brim. But I felt bat claws rake my shoulders. My back.

"They're REAL!" I shrieked. "They're not fakes!"

"Where . . . where is Byron?" someone cried over the screeching of the clawing, biting bats.

"We're all ALONE here!" I screamed in horror. The last words from my mouth as the bats tore at my hair, my clothes . . . my face!

To be continued in . . .

#7 MY FRIENDS CALL ME MONSTER

But first . . .

Before HorrorLand,
another mummy starred in

THE CURSE OF THE MUMMY'S TOMB

Here's a sneak peek
at R.L. Stine's classic bone-chilling prequel.
Now available with exclusive
new bonus features —
including a guide to ancient Egyptian
hieroglyphic symbols!

11

Beaming the light ahead of me on the floor, I ducked my head and began jogging, following the tunnel as it curved sharply to the right.

The floor began to slope upwards. The air became hot and musty smelling. I found myself gasping for breath.

"Uncle Ben!" I called. "Sari!"

They must be around the next curve in the tunnel, I told myself. It hadn't taken me that long to tie my shoelace. They couldn't have gotten that far ahead.

Hearing a sound, I stopped.

And listened.

Silence now.

Was I starting to hear things?

I had a sudden flash: Was this another mean practical joke? Were Sari and Uncle Ben hiding, waiting to see what I'd do?

Was this another lame trick of theirs to frighten me?

It could be. Uncle Ben, I knew, could never resist a practical joke. He had laughed like a hyena when Sari told him how she'd hid in the mummy case and scared about ten years off my life.

Were they both hiding in mummy cases now, just waiting for me to stumble by?

My heart thumped in my chest. Despite the heat of the ancient tunnel, I felt cold all over.

No, I decided. This isn't a practical joke.

Uncle Ben was too serious today, too worried about his stricken workers. Too worried about what we'd told him about Ahmed. He wasn't in any mood for practical jokes.

I began making my way through the tunnel again. As I jogged, my hand brushed against the beeper at my waist.

Should I push it?

No, I decided.

That would only give Sari a good laugh. She'd be eager to tell everyone how I'd started beeping for help after being in the pyramid for two minutes!

I turned the corner. The tunnel walls seemed to close in on me as the tunnel narrowed.

"Sari? Uncle Ben?"

No echo. Maybe the tunnel was too narrow for an echo.

The floor grew harder, less sandy. In the dim yellow light, I could see that the granite walls were lined with jagged cracks. They looked like dark lightning bolts coming down from the ceiling.

"Hey — where *are* you guys?" I shouted.

I stopped when the tunnel branched in two directions.

I suddenly realized how scared I was.

Where had they disappeared to? They *had* to have realized by now that I wasn't with them.

I stared at the two openings, shining my light first into one tunnel, then the other.

Which one had they entered?

Which one?

My heart pounding, I ran into the tunnel on the left and shouted their names.

No reply.

I backed out quickly, my light darting wildly over the floor, and stepped into the tunnel to the right.

This tunnel was wider and higher. It curved gently to the right.

A maze of tunnels. That's how Uncle Ben had described the pyramid. Maybe thousands of tunnels, he had told me.

Thousands.

Keep moving, I urged myself.

Keep moving, Gabe.

They're right up ahead. They've got to be!

I took a few steps and then called out to them.

I heard something.

Voices?

I stopped. It was so quiet now. So quiet, I could hear my heart pounding in my chest.

The sound again.

I listened hard, holding my breath.

It was a chattering sound. A soft chittering. Not a human voice. An insect, maybe. Or a rat.

"Uncle Ben? Sari?"

Silence.

I took a few more steps into the tunnel. Then a few more.

I decided I'd better forget my pride and beep them.

So what if Sari teased me about it?

I was too frightened to care.

If I beeped them, they'd be right there to get me in a few seconds.

But as I reached to my waist for the beeper, I was startled by a loud noise.

The insect chittering became a soft *cracking* sound.

I stopped to listen, the fear rising up to my throat.

The soft cracking grew louder.

It sounded like someone breaking saltines in two.

Only louder. Louder.

Louder.

Right under my feet.

I turned my eyes to the floor.

I shined the light at my shoes.

It took me so long to realize what was happening.

The ancient tunnel floor was cracking apart beneath me.

The cracking grew louder, seemed to come from all directions to surround me.

By the time I realized what was happening, it was too late.

I felt as if I were being pulled down, sucked down by a powerful force.

The floor crumbled away beneath me, and I was falling.

Falling down, down, down an endless black hole.

I opened my mouth to scream, but no sound came out.

My hands flew up and grabbed — nothing!

I closed my eyes and fell.

Down, down into the swirling blackness.

I heard the flashlight clang against the floor.

Then I hit. Hard.

I landed on my side. Pain shot through my body, and I saw red. A flash of bright red that grew brighter and brighter until I had to close my eyes. I think the force of the blow knocked me out for a short while.

When I opened my eyes, everything was a gray-yellow blur. My side ached. My right elbow throbbed with pain.

I tried the elbow. It seemed to move okay.

I sat up. The haze slowly began to lift, like a curtain slowly rising.

Where was I?

A sour smell invaded my nostrils. The smell of decay. Of ancient dust. Of death.

The flashlight had landed beside me on the concrete floor. I followed its beam of light toward the wall.

And gasped.

The light stopped on a hand.

A human hand.

Or was it?

The hand was attached to an arm. The arm hung stiffly from an erect body.

My hand trembling, I grabbed up the flashlight and tried to steady the light on the figure.

It was a mummy, I realized. Standing on its feet near the far wall.

Eyeless, mouthless, the bandaged face seemed to stare back at me, tense and ready, as if waiting for me to make the first move.

About the Author

R.L. Stine's books are read all over the world. So far, his books have sold more than 300 million copies, making him one of the most popular children's authors in history. Besides Goosebumps, R.L. Stine has written the teen series Fear Street and the funny series Rotten School, as well as the Mostly Ghostly series, The Nightmare Room series, and the two-book thriller *Dangerous Girls*. R.L. Stine lives in New York with his wife, Jane, and Minnie, his King Charles spaniel. You can learn more about him at www.RLStine.com.

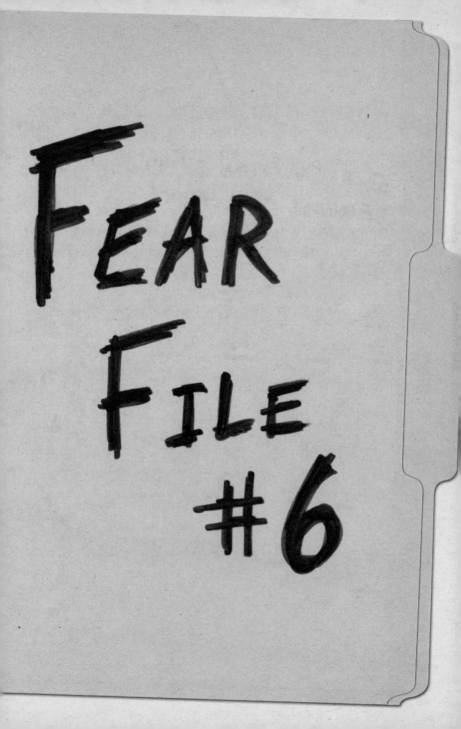

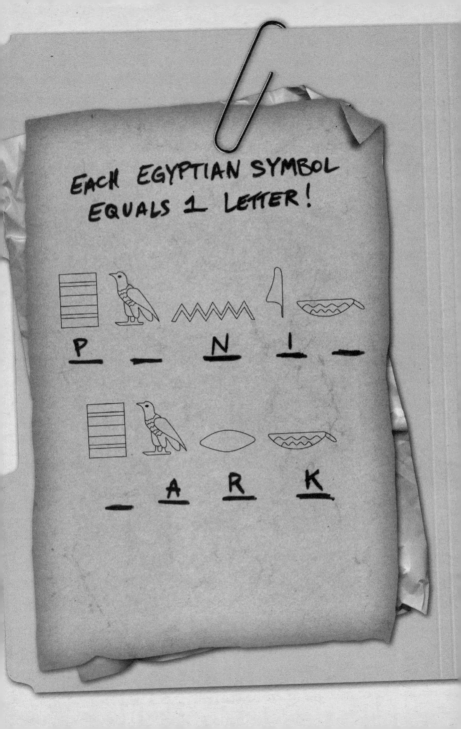

THE TOP TEN SCARIEST RIDES
IN HORRORLAND

#10 Hungry Crocs Piggyback Ride
They're lean, green, and extremely mean.

#9 Bottomless Canoe Ride
Looking for safety? Don't hold your breath!

#8 Landmine Maze
Watch your step. Victory will be yours ... or MINE!

#7 Coffin Cruise
Why not go with the flow? Lie back and relax. Forever.

FIND THE REST at
WWW.ESCAPEHorrorLAND.COM
—LIZZY

MAP #6

↓ Connects to Map #12 ↓

↓ Connects to Map #10 ↓

Before **Goosebumps HorrorLand** there was...

THE ORIGINAL SERIES FROM THE MASTER OF FRIGHT!

Goosebumps®

ONE DAY at HORRORLAND

R.L. STINE

SCHOLASTIC

NOW with BONUS FEATURES!

LOOK in the back of the **BOOK** for exclusive new secrets and clues from your favorite **SCREAM** park

SCHOLASTIC

THIS BOOK IS YOUR TICKET TO

www.EnterHorrorLand.com

CHECKLIST #6

- [ ] The newest HorrorLand rollercoaster isn't scary enough. Can you fix it?

- [ ] But wait! The ride's controls are hidden under the pyramids. Not even the Horrors will go there! Will you?

- [ ] Avoid the creepy Sphinx statues in the Terror Tombs—and don't wake the mummies!

- [ ] Carefully tinker with the circuit-box to restart the ride so it meets all Fright Restrictions.

- [ ] Uh-oh! You didn't just fix the coaster... you awakened the DADDY of all mummies— King Tuttan-Rha!

_____

USER NAME

_____

PASSWORD

NOW WITH BONUS FEATURES!